T0099069

MENINGITIS

MENINGITIS

A Work of Fiction

Yuriy Tarnawsky

All of the characters in this book are fictitious.

First Edition

Library of Congress catalog number: 77-088231
ISNB: 0-914590-48-0 (cloth)
ISBN: 0-914590-49-9 (paper)

Published by FICTION COLLECTIVE
Distributed by George Braziller, Inc.
One Park Avenue
New York, New York 10016

This publication is in part made possible with support from the National Endowment for the Arts in Washington, D.C.

This publication is in part made possible with support from the New York State Council on the Arts.

Grateful acknowledgment is also made for the support of Brooklyn College and Teachers & Writers Collaborative.

TABLE OF CONTENTS

A DAY IN THE LIFE

Jim Morrison woke up. It was quiet in the house and outside. It was dark. Jim Morrison didn't know what time it was. It was a few minutes after three in the morning in reality. Jim Morrison didn't know why he'd awakened. That is he hadn't been awakened by a noise or dream. He lay still for a few seconds. He lay on his back. He felt wide awake. There was no stuffiness in his head as is usual after sleeping. It was as if Jim Morrison had been awake all along. He then sat up. He threw back the blanket. He stood up on the bed. There was a window above the bed. The window was wide. It was short. It was high up. There was a blind on the window. The blind was made from bamboo slats. Jim Morrison pushed back the blind. He leaned his chest on the wall. The wall was made from unfinished wood. Jim Morrison was naked. He felt the texture of the wood on his chest. The splinters of the wood seemed to be trying to push themselves into his flesh. Jim Morrison looked outside. He could see the rushes growing around the house. He could also see the houses around the house. Beyond the houses he could see more rushes and bushes. The sky was lighter than the ground. The sky seemed almost luminous. It was gray. It seemed overcast. The bushes were swaying in the wind. It was only then Jim Morrison noticed the wind. It was as if he were watching a movie. It was as if the sound had been just switched on. Due to the bushes swaying the houses amidst the bushes seemed to sway too. Jim Morrison looked outside for a few seconds. He then decided to get dressed and go out. He moved away from the window. He let the blind down. It struck the wall on being let down. The blind made a light noise. Jim

Morrison got off the bed. There were closets in the room. Jim Morrison remembered which closet his clothes were in. He went to the closet. He tiptoed. He opened the closet. He made practically no noise. He decided to put on swimming trunks, sweat shirt, and pants. He knew where these things were. He found the swimming trunks first. He put them on. Next he found the sweat shirt. He put it on. Finally he found the pants. He put them on. They didn't need a belt. After this Jim Morrison closed the closet. He went to the door. He again tiptoed. He continued tiptoeing from then on. He opened the door. He again made practically no noise. He walked out of the room. He shut the door. He did this in the same way as opening it. He was in a small hallway. It led to a playroom. Jim Morrison went into the playroom. One of the outside doors was in it. Jim Morrison walked to this door. It was locked. The lock was in the doorknob. Jim Morrison turned the door knob. The door opened. There was a wire screen outside the door. The screen wasn't locked. It had a spring attached to it. Jim Morrison pushed open the screen. He stepped outside. He shut the outside door. He made again practically no noise. He held the screen in his hand. He let the screen close. He made again practically no noise. He turned left. He found himself under a porch. He was on the boardwalk leading away from the house. He was facing the boardwalk running past the house. He stood still for a few seconds. He was debating whether to go right or left on coming to the boardwalk running past the house. One could get to the sea going in either direction along the boardwalk running past the house. It was closer to the sea going along the boardwalk to the right. Jim Morrison wanted to get to the sea. He wanted to go east. This direction was to the left. Jim Morrison therefore decided to turn left on the boardwalk running past the house. He walked to the boardwalk. He no longer tiptoed. He made a fair amount of noise while walking. The boards on the boardwalk were new. They were thick. Jim Morrison's footsteps resounded deeply on the boards. The shock of his feet landing on the boards was carried up his legs. Jim Morrison could feel the inside of his chest vibrating from his footsteps. The sensation was similar to a sad emotion. In other words Jim Morrison seemed to be emotionally moved by his footsteps as if by something sad. He turned left on the boardwalk. He continued walking as before. There were bushes and houses on both sides of the boardwalk. The bushes were low. They never rose more than two feet above the sidewalk. The houses were also fairly low. They usually had a single story. They were fairly far away from the boardwalk. Jim Morrison therefore was barely aware of the bushes and houses.

He seemed to be walking in an open field. He still couldn't see the sky very well. He felt however even more certain than in the house the sky was overcast. The clouds seemed to be hanging low. Jim Morrison could now feel the wind. He could feel it primarily on the exposed parts of his body. The wind was fairly cold. It felt pleasant to Jim Morrison however. It felt like a hand comforting him. The hand seemed to give him confidence. The wind was also like comforting words. One had to make a few turns along the boardwalk in order to get to the sea. The boardwalk sloped up a little close to the sea. This was so because of a ridge of dunes running along the sea. There were steps leading down to the beach from the highest point on the boardwalk. Jim Morrison got to the steps. He stopped. He faced the sea. He looked at it. The beach and the sea were dark. They were like the dark part of the negative of a photograph. The surf along the edge of the sea was white. The surf looked like bundles of linen lying in a strip. Jim Morrison looked to his right and left. The surf stretched as far as he could see in both directions. Its movement was noticeable. The sea seemed to be moving the bundles of linen around. The sea seemed to be washing them without having untied them. It was making a fair amount of noise. The noise seemed to consist largely of the phonemes "oo" and "sh." The wind was stronger on top of the steps than on the boardwalk. The wind was coming off the sea. Jim Morrison noticed this only now. He could feel the wind now with the whole of his body. He could feel the wind with the clothed part of his body from the way his clothes were sticking to his body up front. It was as if the front of his body were exerting a gravitational pull on his clothes. It was also as if his clothes were glued to the front of his body. Jim Morrison could feel his hair move in the wind. The hair seemed to be gesticulating like a person in the course of speaking. The person and speech seemed very emotional. Jim Morrison also could feel the wind deforming the flesh on his face. The wind was doing this similarly to deforming his clothes except to a much lesser degree. Jim Morrison decided to walk down to the sea. He walked down the steps. There was more sand on the steps than on the boardwalk. The boards on the steps seemed harder than on the boardwalk. The boards on the steps seemed very new. The sand would form lumps under Jim Morrison's feet. The lumps were very hard. They seemed concrete. They hurt Jim Morrison's feet. Jim Morrison stepped off the steps onto the beach. The sand on the beach seemed extremely soft. The sand seemed an unmade bed. The linen on the bed seemed tousled. The sand was cold on the surface. The sand was quite warm underneath however. Jim

Morrison found this pleasant. The wind was weaker on the beach than on the steps. Jim Morrison walked to the sea. The wind got stronger on the edge of the sea. The wind seemed even stronger there than at the top of the steps. Jim Morrison had trouble breathing at times. The sand along the edge of the sea was wet. The sand was smooth. It seemed as hard as concrete. This was before the sand would break up under Jim Morrison's feet. It would then seem soft again. It wouldn't feel as soft however as where it was dry. The sea would wash over Jim Morrison's feet from time to time. The water was warm. It seemed to fit over Jim Morrison's feet like shoes. The shoes seemed rubber. They actually seemed galoshes. The surf seemed even whiter from up close than from the top of the stairs. Jim Morrison seemed to be standing in a lit area. Because of this the rest of the world seemed darker to him than before. He seemed to be able to distinguish hardly anything beyond the line of the surf. He walked around in a small area for a few minutes. He then began walking east. He walked along the wet part of the sand. The surf would sometimes reach his feet. Jim Morrison tried not to let this happen. He'd try to move up on the beach at those times. He wasn't always successful in this. He held his hands in his pockets. He kept his shoulders hunched up. He kept his head bent down a little. He did all this because of the wind. He felt cold. He'd look up from time to time. He noticed the topography on his left. There were dunes on his left. Houses stuck up in places over the dunes. The houses were dark. Jim Morrison saw them. They seemed railroad cars. The cars seemed freight. They seemed to be moving. The train seemed very long. Jim Morrison also felt he was a train moving along the beach. There was a long row of houses in one area. Jim Morrison passed them. He knew there wouldn't be any houses for a long distance. He knew there would be only two areas with houses within the next three or so miles. The first one was within about half a mile. There were three houses there. The second one was within the next quarter of a mile. There was one house there. The house was actually only a shack. Jim Morrison watched for the houses to appear. He passed the group of houses and the shack. The houses and the shack were just as dark as the preceding houses. Jim Morrison knew there wouldn't be any houses for as far as he planned to go. He continued walking. He wanted to get to a place another mile or so beyond the shack. He felt he'd walked that distance. He stopped. There were still dunes on his left. They were about fifty yards from the sea. The dunes were quite tall. They were about twenty feet tall. The dunes were steep. They had grass growing on top of them. There was a wildlife preserve behind them. Jim

Morrison could see them quite clearly. This was so even though it was just as dark as when he'd left the house. He felt he could see the grass on top of the dunes. It wasn't certain this was so. Jim Morrison turned toward the sea. He looked at it. It looked a little different than when he'd come up to it first. It looked less dark in the distance and less white near the shore. This was due to Jim Morrison's having gotten used to the darkness. Jim Morrison looked at the sea for about five minutes. He stood a few feet above the line of the surf. The tide was rising. A few splashes of water fell on Jim Morrison's feet. Jim Morrison decided to move back. There was a ridge in the sand about five feet back. Jim Morrison turned around. He climbed onto the ridge. He went about another two feet back. He faced the sea. He sat down. The sand felt cold to his seat and feet. The sand felt damp. It felt also hard. Jim Morrison pushed the top layer of sand out from under his seat and feet. The sand underneath felt warmer, dry and soft. It felt like soft bedlinen. Jim Morrison sat with his knees drawn up a little. He covered his feet with the sand. They felt warm. Jim Morrison clasped his arms around his knees. He felt warm all over. He felt comfortable. He proceeded sitting in this position. He looked at the sea. He could see the sea and sky. For a few minutes the sky and sea looked to him as from where he'd been standing. Then however they began to grow lighter. This wasn't merely due to Jim Morrison's eyes getting used to the sea and sky. The sea and sky were actually growing lighter. This was due to the rotation of the earth. Jim Morrison merely noticed it now because of having started to concentrate on the sea and sky. The process of growing lighter was very slow. Jim Morrison however seemed to be aware of it continually. The sea and sky were getting lighter from his left. This was in the east. Jim Morrison seemed like an extremely precise light meter perceiving the very minute increase in light and gradation from the left to the right. This ability of his seemed to be due to his position and his sitting still. At one point the sky got light enough for Jim Morrison to see the sea clearly. In other words he was now able to see every detail of the sea his eyes were able to perceive with any light intensity. This was so even though the sky was still not as light as it was going to get eventually. It was then gray. It seemed low. It seemed overcast. It seemed it was going to rain. Jim Morrison felt disappointed by this. The sky however proceeded getting lighter. At one point some blue became visible in the sky. This was shortly before the sunrise. It was clear then to Jim Morrison the sky was clear. The air was merely misty. This was the reason for the stars not having been visible. Now the mist was dissipating with the appearance of the sun. Along about then the sky in the east began to turn rosy. After that the sky above didn't seem to change color for a long time. The sky continued grayish-blue. Jim Morrison kept looking to his left. The sky in that direction continued getting rosier. Now a good portion of the sky in that direction was rosy. Then at one point Jim Morrison saw a flash of light. The flash seemed white. Jim Morrison was practically blinded by it. It was like a burst of flames burning out his eyes. The flash also seemed painful. It was like the stab of a needle. The flash lasted a fraction of a second. The flash was obviously the sun appearing. It was however as if the sun had sunken back behind the horizon after having appeared for a fraction of a second. This actually seemed to have happened. It seemed the earth on the horizon was moving up and down thus having permitted the sun to be visible for a fraction of a second. In this the earth seemed a branch swaying. It also seemed the earth was possibly oscillating while rotating. The earth seemed to have moved in a clockwise direction while the sun had disappeared. A few seconds after having disappeared the sun reappeared. It reappeared again in the form of a flash. This flash was not as bright as the first one. Jim Morrison saw this flash also. It however didn't affect his eyes as strongly as the first one. This was due to his eyes having been conditioned to light by the first flash. The sun didn't disappear after the second flash. The sun seemed to remain stationary for a few seconds after having reappeared. It looked like a blinding-white cusp of fire lying with its convex side up on the horizon. The sun then proceeded to protrude gradually more from behind the horizon. The sun seemed to be doing this now without any pause. The sun also seemed to be doing this faster than the rotation of the earth warranted. The sun seemed to be coming out of the earth like a turd out of a man's anus. Jim Morrison thought of this image. He didn't find it unpleasant. On the contrary, he found it pleasant. This was due to the image's stressing the naturalness of the act of sunrise. It seemed the earth was relieving itself of the sun. It seemed the earth was feeling a relief at this. The sun continued seeming to rise faster than the rotation of the earth warranted after rising above the horizon. The color of the sun changed then. The sun became whiter. It seemed a reflection of a very bright object on a fairly reflective surface. The sun also no longer seemed as round as while rising above the horizon. The shape of the sun seemed irregular. The shape seemed to change somewhat. This seemed to be happening as in the case of the reflection of a bright object on a fairly reflective but not perfectly even surface. The sun continued seeming to rise faster than the rotation of the earth warranted until coming about to the zenith. The color of the sky changed on the sun's rising above the horizon. The color of the sky continued to change a little after that. The sky turned progressively more blue. Eventually it became very blue. It however didn't seem to be uniformly blue. There seemed to be darker and lighter areas in it. In this it seemed like a surface painted with a thin coat of paint. The color of the sea also changed on the sun's rising above the horizon. The color of the sea also continued to change for a while. The color of the sea continued to change a little longer than that of the sky. The sea also turned progressively bluer. It eventually turned a darker shade of blue than the sky. The sea also seemed to be uniformly blue. This was so in spite of its reflecting the sun in places, undulating with waves, and rippling in the wind. The sea also seemed to have risen a little. It seemed to have grown more convex. It seemed to have grown very convex. The portion of the sea halfway between the shore and the horizon seemed to be much higher than that along the shore and the horizon. In this the sea seemed to be a large pool of mercury. The sea seemed very heavy because of that. The action of the surf along the edge of the beach seemed like that of hands. They seemed small. They seemed blue. They seemed to try to modify the shape of the beach. They seemed to belong to the sea. There seemed to be a large number of them. The number however didn't seem exorbitant. The number seemed normal as two hands are normal for a person. The wind died down a little after the sun's rising above the horizon. The wind turned to a breeze. The breeze eventually grew warmer. The warmth in the breeze was like a fragrance. The breeze seemed like a ladies' thin garment impregnated with perfume. Jim Morrison enjoyed feeling the breeze on his face. Soon after the sunrise some birds appeared around him. Actually, they had been there all along. Jim Morrison merely didn't notice them. Also, they began to move then. Until then they'd been sitting still. They were sandpipers and gulls. They began to walk and fly. They were looking for food. Some of the gulls also sat on the water. They did this beyond the breaking waves. The gulls stayed mostly by themselves. They walked fairly slowly. They flew with powerful sweeps of their wings. Some of the gulls flew far away. Others came from far away. The gulls sometimes made noises. The noises were loud. They were unpleasant. They were a little like those of geese. The noises were also like the screeching of rusty hinges. Occasionally one of the gulls would eat something. Jim Morrison could never tell what it was. He also could never see where the gull had gotten it. He'd notice the gull only after its starting to eat. The sandpipers stayed together. They mostly walked. They seemed to be gathered into military formations. The sandpipers walked very fast. Their legs and feet were very thin. Jim Morrison could barely see the legs and feet even when the sandpipers didn't move. While the sandpipers were moving their legs were but a faint blur. It was like a shadow falling onto glass or clear water. The sandpipers also flew in formations. The beating of the sandpiper's wings was also very fast. The wings also seemed a blur. It seemed a moving butterfly. The sandpipers would usually fly some fifty feet. The sandpipers seemed to feel their food was distributed about fifty feet apart. The sandpipers walked about another fifty feet. The sandpipers were pecking all the time while walking. They seemed to be eating all the time. Jim Morrison also couldn't see what they were eating. Whatever it was it was obviously very small. Jim Morrison had a feeling it was sand. This was partly due to the sandpipers' name. It was also partly due to the sandpipers' being small. The birds weren't afraid of Jim Morrison. They seemed to be unaware of him. This was even during his moving. Jim Morrison would occasionally move a little hoping to evoke the birds' reaction. Their behavior seemed to be due to his having appeared on the scene before sunrise. It was as if it were a proof of his not having hostile intentions toward them. After about an hour past the sunrise Jim Morrison noticed fish in the water. He noticed them accidentally. He was staring absentmindedly at the surf. At one instant he saw the profile of a fish. The fish was fairly long. It was shaped like an eye. The fish was dark gray. It was almost blue. It was about the color of lead. The fish was like an eye. The eye seemed to be staring at Jim Morrison. It seemed friendly. It seemed to belong to the sea. The wave in which the fish was located was curved at the top. The wave looked like an eyelid without the fish. The wave looked completely like an eyelid with the fish. The eyelid also seemed that of the sea. After seeing the fish Jim Morrison noticed more fish. This was undoubtedly due to his having seen the first fish. Jim Morrison had become sensitive to the fish. Some of them were shaped differently than the first fish. They were smaller or larger for instance. They were also rounder or thinner. Their color also differed sometimes from that of the first fish and from each other. The color could be black, green, silver and white for instance. All the fish seemed eyes. The eyes seemed the same as the first one. Jim Morrison then began to feel the sea had very many eyes. He felt this was appropriate. This seemed to be due to the size of the sea. In seeming to have eyes the sea was as in seeming to have hands. The sun continued rising. Jim Morrison was aware of this. This made him aware of the passage of time. He knew sooner or later people would come his way. This worried him. He kept looking for people. This was especially true of the west. Jim Morrison strained his eyes. He however could see no trace of people. The beach on the horizon was indistinct. The beach there seemed a cloud of vapor. The cloud seemed tiny. While doing this Jim Morrison heard at one point the sound of a car engine. The sound came from his left rear. The sound was soft. It was like a person's humming. The sound should have been soothing therefore. It frightened Jim Morrison however. He jerked. He turned his head in the direction of the sound. He saw a car driving along the beach. The car was about fifty feet away. Cars were allowed on that beach. The cars allowed on the beach were taxis only however. The car therefore was a taxi. It was fairly big. It was a station wagon. It was red and white. It didn't have any special taxi markings on it. Its windows were dark. Jim Morrison couldn't see very well inside the car. He could see the outline of its driver however. Jim Morrison couldn't distinguish the driver's features very well. He could only tell the driver was male and white. On the car's getting closer Jim Morrison could hear the sound of its wheels on the sand. The sound was sibilant. It seemed ominous. The wheels seemed to be devouring sand. They seemed to be doing this with great relish. The car continued moving. Soon it passed out of the range of Jim Morrison's sight. To see the car Jim Morrison would have had to turn his head right. He however didn't do it. He continued looking at the sea. The sun continued rising. Jim Morrison still couldn't see any people on the horizon on the right however. He was pleased by it. He began to feel no one would appear there during the whole day. He did this in spite of knowing this was highly unlikely. Then at one point he heard the sound of human voices. The sound came also from his rear left. Jim Morrison turned his head in the direction of the sound. He saw two men walking. They were middle-aged. They were dressed as fishermen. They wore rubber boots. The boots reached up to the crotch. The men carried fishing tackle. They didn't seem to notice Jim Morrison. He turned his head back soon after seeing them. He heard them pass behind his back. He heard their footsteps. The footsteps were like labored breathing. It seemed to be due to an illness. The men talked. They did this very sporadically however. Thus in the course of passing behind Jim Morrison's back they exchanged not more than a dozen words. Jim Morrison heard the men talking. He couldn't distinguish the words however. They seemed a part of the noise the men made while walking. The men passed behind Jim Morrison's back. They continued walking. Eventually Jim Morrison could see them without having to turn his head very far to the right. Eventually they disappeared from his range of sight. Jim Morrison wasn't sure whether they were coming from or going fishing. Soon thereafter he saw a dot on the horizon on the right. The dot was dark. It grew. It was obviously a person walking. The person was walking in Jim Morrison's direction. From then on Jim Morrison paid little attention to the sea, sky and sun. He kept looking at the person. The person became progressively more distinct. At first Jim Morrison thought the person was a woman. Then he thought the person was a man. Finally Jim Morrison realized the person was a woman. The woman was actually a girl. She seemed in her mid twenties. She wore a scarf, sweater and slacks. She walked along the edge of the beach. She walked fairly fast. She was apparently going somewhere. In other words she didn't seem to be merely strolling. This was probably the reason for her walking along the edge of the surf. The sand was hard there. The girl could walk faster there than higher up on the beach. She greeted Jim Morrison on coming close to him. He answered the greeting. He felt a little better on being greeted. The girl passed him. He didn't follow her with his eyes. Soon thereafter he saw two dots on the horizon on the right. They were also dark. They also grew. They were also obviously persons. The persons were walking in Jim Morrison's direction. From then on Jim Morrison kept looking at the persons. He felt uneasy. He felt threatened. It was as if a heavy object were suspended above his head. It was as if the object could fall on Jim Morrison. Fairly soon after his noticing the two persons another person emerged from behind the two. That person was moving in a different way. The person was moving from side to side. Jim Morrison realized the person was running. The sight of the person and the realization upset Jim Morrison. Jim Morrison decided to move from the beach. He decided to move to the dunes. He got up. He felt very stiff. He turned around. He nearly fell over from the stiffness. He steadied himself. He began walking toward the dunes. He did this very slowly at first. He tried to do it gradually faster. He tried to loosen up this way. About halfway between the edge of the beach and the dunes he felt practically normal. He then began running. He ran also gradually faster. After a few steps he ceased accelerating however. Even at that point he wasn't running very fast however. He reached the dunes at this speed. He continued running. He ran still at the same speed. He began ascending the dune. It was very steep. The sand kept falling on Jim Morrison's legs. It was warm. It felt like long straight hair. The hair seemed a woman's. Jim Morrison found running up the dune very strenuous. He began slowing down. Soon he was no longer running. He was climbing very laboriously. He moved this way up the rest of the dune. He got to the top of the dune. The dune went down fairly sharply on the other side. Jim Morrison descended down the other side of the dune a few feet. He then turned around. He looked at the running man. The man was still a long distance away. Jim Morrison decided to watch the man. Soon Jim Morrison began to be able to distinguish the man's features. The man was of medium height. He was very muscular. He was well proportioned however. Because of this he looked slender in spite of being muscular. His hair was fairly long. Jim Morrison wasn't sure whether the hair was all gone or not on top. This was due to the color of the hair. The hair was brown. It was bleached by the sun however. The hair was golden in places. The man's skin was tanned. It was also golden. The skin on the man's forehead was nearly the same color as the bleached hair. The man wore a pair of swimming trunks only. They were of the bikini type. They were bright blue. They contrasted sharply with the man's skin. The man wore also sunglasses. They were of the aviator type. The man ran effortlessly. He seemed an experienced runner. His face was impassive. It was almost like that of a man asleep. This seemed to indicate the man liked running. His mouth was slightly open. Its inside was dark. The man seemed to be holding the darkness like an object in his mouth. He seemed to be feeding on the darkness. It seemed a piece of candy. The man seemed to be enjoying the darkness like a piece of candy. The skin on his cheeks could be seen expanding and contracting during the breathing. The skin seemed a membrane. The membrane seemed to be causing the breathing. In other words the man seemed to be breathing because of the skin on his cheeks expanding and contracting. His muscles rippled. This was especially true of the pectorals. The movement was very graceful. It was like the sound of a harpsichord. The man carried his arms very low. His hands were on the level of his hips. This also seemed to indicate the man was an experienced runner. His stride was long. His feet seemed to be taking off the ground by themselves. They seemed two birds. The birds seemed pigeons. This was probably due to the size and color of the man's feet. The feet were white. The man seemed to be pursuing his feet like two doves. He seemed to want to catch the doves. He didn't seem to be able to do it. The length of his stride also seemed to indicate he was an experienced runner. He continued getting closer to Jim Morrison. The man didn't seem to have noticed Jim Morrison. At one point Jim Morrison decided to stop looking at the man. It was as if Jim Morrison were afraid of the man's proximity. He turned right. His back was now turned to the sea. There was grass growing on the other side of the dune. The grass was very sparse close to the top of the dune. The grass got progressively thicker down the dune. At one point down the dune there was a hollow place. The place was completely devoid of grass. The place looked like a nest of sand. The place looked very comfortable. Jim Morrison decided to settle in that place. He walked down the dune. The sand escaped from under his feet. It seemed tears rolling out from under a person's eyelids. Jim Morrison's feet seemed the eyelids. Jim Morrison got down into the hollow place. He sat down. He sat down in the same position as on the beach. He faced away from the sea. As was said, the area beyond the dunes constituted a wildlife preserve. It extended for miles in both directions. It was overgrown with grass, bushes, and trees. The grass was sparse. It was silver-gray. The bushes were thick. They were low. They were dark green. They looked like pubic hair. The hair seemed a woman's. This was due to a woman's pubic hair being bushier than a man's. There were very few trees. They grew in groups. The trees were sparse even in groups. The trees were low. They were dwarfed. Their trunks were gnarled. The trees were mostly pines and oaks. There was water on the other side of the preserve. The water was that of a sound. The distance from Jim Morrison to the sound was about half a mile. He could see the sound. The water in the sound was calm. The water was blue. The sound was about two miles wide. The land on the other side of the sound was covered with houses and trees. There were houses to the left and right of the preserve. The houses to the left were more numerous. They could be barely seen. This was due primarily to the distance. This was also partly due to the visibility. It was hazy. The haze was bluish. Jim Morrison wasn't aware of the haze until now. The air around him seemed perfectly clear. There was a breeze. The grass around Jim Morrison was swaying. It did this like jets of water in a fountain. Jim Morrison could almost hear the grass making the sound of water. He could also feel the breeze on his face. The breeze felt pleasant. This was due to the sunshine being strong. It burned Jim Morrison's face. The breeze was cooling off his face. Jim Morrison was looking straight ahead. There was a glare above the sand. Jim Morrison could feel the glare around his face. The glare was like cotton around his face. Jim Morrison seemed to be looking out of the glare as if out of a ball of cotton. Everything shimmered in the sunlight. The grass and bushes looked like water shining. They had a bluish tinge. The water in the sound shimmered also. The air itself, finally, shimmered also. This seemed especially so because of the bluish haze. Jim Morrison wondered if the running man would be coming back. Jim Morrison didn't look out from behind the dune to check this. He therefore never found this out. While sitting, he heard noises from the beach. They seemed those of cars and people. The noises weren't very numerous. Only at one point were there many noises. They were those of people's voices. It'd sounded as if a large group of people were walking by then. They seemed to be walking east. They didn't seem to have returned. That is, no group of people had walked toward the west talking. Jim Morrison felt thirsty and hungry while sitting. The thirst was unpleasant. It seemed a sin weighing on Jim Morrison's soul. The hunger was pleasant. It seemed a right decision Jim Morrison was carrying out. His face burned from the sun and wind. The skin on his face seemed too tight for his face. Or, rather, his face seemed too big for his skin. His face also seemed uncomfortable. It was as if it were too hard. Jim Morrison's face seemed like a coffin too tight and hard for Jim Morrison. At one point he had to urinate. He got up. He felt stiff. He stretched himself. He walked a few yards down the dune. He urinated. He did this onto the sand. He urinated in one spot. The urine made a hole in the sand. The urine foamed in the hole. The urine was white. There seemed to be a spring in the sand. The water seemed to be coming out of the spring in the spot Jim Morrison urinated at. After urinating he returned to his former spot. He sat down in it as before. He remained in this position for a long time. The sun kept moving across the sky. The sun sank to about half-way between the zenith and the horizon. It turned cooler. The wind changed direction. The wind now blew from the west. It became very hazy. The sunlight changed color. The sunlight became orange. It seemed visible in the air. The sunlight seemed an orange tent. The tent seemed silk. Its peak seemed the sun. The tent seemed to be centered around Jim Morrison. There were no noises of cars or people coming from the beach any more. Jim Morrison decided to go back to the beach. He got up. He again felt very stiff. He again nearly fell over. He steadied himself. He began to stretch gently. He loosened up. He felt very weak. This made him perceive the world differently. He felt indifferent about it. He felt nothing mattered in the end. He climbed to the top of the dune. He found the climb laborious. He stopped at the top of the dune. He looked at the sea. A mist hung over the beach and sea. The mist was very blue. It was almost opaque. It looked like ink vapor. The ink seemed to be boiled. It seemed to be boiled in the sea. It was as if the sea were a cauldron. The beach was deserted. It shone in the sunlight. The beach seemed a road. The road seemed paved. Jim Morrison descended from the dune. He walked to his previous spot. He didn't feel like sitting down there. He decided to stand. He looked at the sea. He looked toward the east and west. He then began to walk. He walked about ten paces east and west from his original spot. The sun was sinking now rapidly. The mist on the horizon was very thick. The sun turned red. It seemed huge. It seemed to have grown in the course of the day. The sun seemed to have done this like a fruit. The fruit seemed to have been ripening. This seemed especially so due to the red color. There were apparently clouds above the horizon. They weren't visible through the mist. This was apparent for the following reason. While still quite a distance above the horizon the lower part of the sun became invisible. The sun proceeded to descend behind this layer of clouds. The sun again seemed to do this faster than travelling across most of the sky. Eventually the sun disappeared completely. At this point the wind got stronger. At one point the wind filled Jim Morrison's mouth so much Jim Morrison lost his breath. His mouth seemed a sail filled with wind. It seemed Jim Morrison would move like a sail boat. The light didn't change noticeably for a while after the sun's setting. This surprised Jim Morrison. With time however the light began to change. The sky in the east began to grow dark. The sky was growing bluer. The sky seemed to be doing this in one area only. The area seemed round. It looked like a bruise. It seemed the sky was growing dark in the east because of having been hit. The sky seemed in this a human being. Eventually the blue area widened to the whole eastern part of the sky. The sky then no longer seemed bruised. The blue area began to spread west. It was doing this quite fast. It was wide. It seemed a bird flying west. The bird seemed enormous. It seemed benevolent. It was clear it was the night. Jim Morrison suspected no more people would appear on the beach that day. He was hoping to be wrong. He turned out to be right however. He was disappointed by this. The wind kept rising. Now the whole space between the dunes and the sea seemed filled with the wind like a sail. It seemed the whole area would start moving like a sail boat. It seemed a storm was coming. Jim Morrison felt dejected because of this. He felt insignificant. He felt helpless. He felt like a drop of rain trembling on a branch in the wind. He sat down in his original spot. He sat in the same position as before. The dark area in the sky kept moving gradually until covering about two thirds of the sky. The whole sky then turned dark. While this happened the area no longer seemed a bird. The area also no longer seemed benevolent. After the sky's getting dark the earth began to get dark too. This really seemed to be happening in this sequence. The air above the ground seemed to be filling with black gas. The gas seemed the vapor of black ink. With the earth's becoming dark the stars became visible. They grew progressively more numerous. They also grew brighter. Eventually they seemed lines. The lines could have been dotted lines. They seemed to be those of a drawing in a blueprint. The drawing seemed that of the universe. The lines also could have been solid. They seemed the skeleton of a structure. The structure could have been a vast hangar. The structure also seemed the universe. The stars thus seemed a blueprint of the universe and the universe at the same time. There didn't seem anything unusual about this. Jim Morrison became moved by the sight of the stars. He was oppressed by the vastness of the structure they seemed to outline. He felt cold. He also felt terribly hungry and thirsty. He felt tiny because of these feelings. He embraced his knees stronger. He buried his face between his knees and arms. He felt very sad. He began crying. He cried quietly. He made hardly any noise. He also made hardly any movement. His tears seemed to be coming out of his eyes without being caused by an emotion. His crying was like a completely dispassionate description of a painful event. The description seemed to be written down. The description seemed to be especially painful because of being dispassionate. Eventually Jim Morrison stopped crying. He didn't know how long he'd cried. He'd cried for about fifteen minutes. He lifted his head. He looked at the sea and sky. They were the same as before. Jim Morrison felt the same as before without having an urge to cry. He realized he'd feel this way for the rest of his life. He could feel his body stiffening from the prolonged motionlessness. The sensation was painful. It was analogous to the chafing of a rock in one's shoe. It was as if Jim Morrison's soul were chafing his body like a rock the foot in a shoe. Jim Morrison wanted to get rid of the sensation. That is he wanted to get rid of his soul as if of a rock in a shoe. He however decided against it. He decided to retain the feeling. In this he seemed to be exercising his will power. That is it was as if he could have gotten rid of his soul at will. In this he also seemed to be punishing himself. Eventually the air grew misty. The mist obscured the stars. The sea and sky then were the same as when Jim Morrison had gone out of the house the night before. For a long time nothing seemed to be changing. Even the thoughts in Jim Morrison's mind didn't progress in one direction. They seemed to be repeating themselves like the surf. This was probably due to Jim Morrison's being constantly aware of the surf. Jim Morrison grew sleepy. He fought the desire to sleep. He was successful in this. That is he didn't fall asleep. With time the darkness began to decrease. The sky became progressively lighter. Eventually it got quite light. Looking at the sky Jim Morrison had a feeling it was already daylight. It was still half an hour till sunrise. The sky was gray. It seemed low. It seemed overcast. It seemed it was going to rain.

WEEKEND

(END OF THE WEEK/END OF THE WORLD)

1. *GOD IS A WOMAN*

George parks his car in the municipal parking lot. There's no fee for parking in the lot. Two spaces to the left of George's car a woman parks her car at the same time as George. There's a sticker on the rear bumper of her car. The sticker says "GOD IS A WOMAN." George gets his suitcase. He gets out of the car. He locks it. He checks all the doors. They're locked. The woman gets out of the car a little before George. She's in her late fifties. She's dumpy. George assumes she's a rabid feminist. He starts walking toward the ferry. The distance is a little over a mile. To get to the ferry George has to turn right. The woman walks in the same direction as he. She has a lead of about ten yards on him. She carries a small bag. George's suitcase is fairly heavy. George doesn't walk very fast because of that. The woman walks just a shade slower than he. He passes her. She speeds up a little. She continues walking a few yards behind George. This goes on for about half a mile. George assumes the woman is going to the same ferry as he. He decides to ask her some questions. This is so in spite of his not liking feminists. He slows down. The woman catches up with him. He asks if she's going to Fire Island. She answers in the affirmative. George is going to Ocean Beach. He asks if the woman is going to Ocean Beach. She answers in the negative. She says she's going to Kismet. She explains where Kismet is in relation to Ocean Beach. She says she'll have to take a different ferry than the one to Ocean Beach. She asks if George is going to Ocean Beach. He answers in the affirmative. He then corrects himself. He's actually going to Robin's Rest. Robin's Rest is near Ocean Beach. To get to Robin's Rest one has to take the Ocean Beach ferry. George says he's going to Robin's Rest. He's been afraid Robin's Rest is a homosexual community. He asks if Robin's Rest is a homosexual community. The woman answers in the negative. She says Cherry Grove and Fire Island Pines are homosexual communities. George has known this. He feels relieved. He tells the woman about his allayed fear. He laughs. The woman reassures him again. He explains he's going to spend the weekend at a beach house. He says he found out about the house through a newspaper. He says he might take a share in the house. The woman says she's going to stay at some friends' house. She says she's meeting her husband there. She says they'll be sailing. She says they own a boat. She says her husband had gone out to the island in the boat. George is surprised a little by her being married. This is due to the sticker on her car. George had suspected the woman to be a lesbian in addition to a rabid feminist. They come to the road he has to take to get to his ferry. The road branches off to the left. The woman says her ferry is straight ahead. George and the woman say good-bye to each other. She wishes him a happy weekend. He wishes her a happy weekend in return.

2. *A BEER*

The road leading to the ferry runs past a parking lot. The lot is full. This is the primary reason for George's having parked his car so far away.—He'd driven up to this parking lot before. Another reason is his wanting to save money. Parking in the lot near the ferry is expensive. The cars in the lot glitter. George doesn't like this. The cars remind him of insects. He gets to the ferry. He goes to the ticket office. He inquires about the ferry to Ocean Beach. He's told the ferry leaves in about half an hour. He buys a round trip ticket to Ocean Beach. It's hot. George is thirsty. He decides to get something to drink. There's a restaurant across the road from the ticket office. The restaurant is in the ferry grounds. George goes there. He decides to get a bottle of beer. He does this. He pays eighty cents for the beer. He finds the price very expensive. He's angry. He takes the bottle. He goes out. He goes back to the ticket office. There are benches next to the office. There's a roof over them. There's a breeze. George stands next to one of the benches. It's empty. George's suitcase is next to George on the ground. He stands drinking the beer. He's sweaty. He doesn't sit down because of this. He wants his legs and back to dry off. He goes on drinking the beer. It tastes good. With time George strays off from the bench. He moves around a little. He doesn't move more than six feet away from the suitcase however. He keeps an eye on the suitcase. He's afraid the suitcase will be stolen. This is so in spite of there being just a few people around. Most of the time George looks across the parking lot. From this direction the cars also glitter. Now they don't look unpleasant to George however. This is due to their being farther away. The cars no longer seem insects. The cars seem to shimmer like a great body of water. The sky is pale blue. There's a trash can near George. On finishing the beer he throws the bottle into the can.

3. *L'AVVENTURA*

The boat leaves at eleven-forty. It's big. It has two levels. It's white. The trip reminds George of the film *L'Avventura.* There's a mist over the water. This mist is especially noticeable on the horizon. The mist is purplish. The contours of the land on the horizon aren't distinct. It's possible therefore to imagine the land looking like Italy. George sits on the upper level. He sits on a bench. He sits on the left side of the boat. Most of the benches are taken. There are three persons sitting on the bench opposite George's on the right side of the boat. The persons are two men and a woman. The men are black. The woman is white. She sits between the two men. She's friendly with them. At the beginning she seems friendlier to one of them. George assumes she belongs to the man. She then seems friendlier to the other man. She and the second man hold hands. George then assumes she belongs to the second man. The thought crosses George's mind she could belong to both men. He feels this isn't so however. This is so because from then on the woman behaves much friendlier to the second man than the first. The second man also behaves as though she belonged to him. He puts his arm around her for instance. George is confused. At one point he hears very clearly the woman speaking. This is due to a gust of wind blowing his way. George notices the woman has a foreign accent. He explains the fact of her being with the black men by her being foreign. He feels the woman wouldn't do this being an American. This obviously isn't so however. George is thinking of the racial situation of a few years ago.

4. *YELLOW MELLOW*

The boat docks. George takes his suitcase. He waits for his turn to get off the boat. He gets off the boat. There's a terminal at the dock. The terminal looks like a warehouse. One has to pass through the terminal to get to the village. George passes through the terminal. The light inside it makes it seem as if it were cloudy outside. There's a policeman standing outside the terminal. He's standing in its shadow. He therefore seems to be standing still inside the terminal. George is going to a house called Yellow Mellow. He asks the policeman directions for getting to Robin's Rest. The policeman tells George to turn left, go to the next major street, turn right, and continue as far as possible. George thanks the policeman. George follows the policeman's directions. He passes a church in the major street. This street ends at another street. One has to turn left or right. George is confused. There've been people walking ahead of him. They turn right. George follows them. He assumes they might be going to Robin's Rest. There's a path going off to the left about thirty feet past the turn. The people don't take that path. George however suspects he should. This is so because of the path's leading in the same direction as the major street. George turns left. The streets until now have been paved with concrete. The path is unpaved. It's covered with sand. There's only a thin layer of sand on the path. The ground underneath the sand is hard. The path winds through tall reeds. At times George is unable to see much more than about a dozen yards ahead and behind. Coming out from behind one turn George sees a girl. She's in her early twenties. George finds her attractive from behind. He's walking much faster than she. He catches up with her very soon. He sees her face. He finds the girl even more attractive now. He greets her. She greets him back. She does this in a fairly unfriendly way. George had planned to talk to her. Her manner of answering makes him change his mind. He speeds up. Very soon thereafter the path ends. It stops at a fence. The fence is broken. There's a hole in it. The fence is in the back of a row of houses. There's some garbage strewn on the ground at the end of the path. George stops. He's confused again. He thinks he must have taken a wrong turn somewhere. He turns around. He sees no other way of proceeding however. He's hoping the girl will come along. He waits a while. The girl doesn't appear however. George assumes she must have taken the turn he'd missed. He doesn't remember a wide path branching off from the one he'd walked along. He assumes the path branching off must have been very narrow. He turns around. He can see beyond the houses. There seems to be a clearing beyond them. George decides to get past them. He goes through the hole in the fence. This leads him between two houses. He continues walking. He sees a street just beyond the houses. It's paved with concrete. George gets to the street. He stops. He looks around. He'd like to ask someone where Yellow Mellow is. There's no one around however. George thinks what to do. He knows what yellow mellow means. He suspects the name of the house is a pun however. He suspects the house is yellow. He looks for a yellow house in the street. There's one on the opposite side of the street a few houses to his left. George walks to the house. There's a sign on it saying "YELLOW MELLOW."

5. *HOWIE*

The house has a porch in front. The porch is open. George gets up onto it. The boards bend under his feet. The boards creak. The house therefore seems run down. This is so in spite of its looking quite new. George comes up to the front door. There's a screen on it. The door is open. The screen is closed. George knocks on the side of it. He peers in through the screen. He sees nobody inside. There's no answer to his knocking. George knocks again. He continues peering in through the screen. There's no answer again to his knocking. George calls out: "Is anybody home?" into the house. He continues peering in through the screen. There's no answer to his calling. George decides to go into the house. He opens the screen. He goes into the house. He closes the screen. He's in the living room. There are two sofas, two armchairs, two lamp tables, two lamps, and a coffee table there. There are various objects scattered over the floor and furniture. Some of the objects are books, magazines, towels, and bathing suits. George puts his suitcase down close to the center of the room. His arm is tired from having carried the suitcase. George notices this only now. It's the right arm. George walks around the room. He looks around. He doesn't know what to do. There's a dining room next to the living room. There's no wall between the two rooms. There's a table, five chairs, and a dresser in the dining room. The dining room is small. The furniture practically fills it. There's a kitchen off the dining room. There's a door leading from the dining room to the kitchen. George peers into the kitchen from the living room. He sees a refrigerator and stove there. They're old-fashioned. They're white. George goes into the dining room. He goes into the kitchen. There's no one there either. There's a sink and cabinet there. They're next to each other. They're also white. There are a few dishes in the sink. They're dirty. There are many dishes piled up on top of the counter. These dishes are clean. They're wet. They must have been stacked recently. There's a door leading outside from the kitchen. There's a sundeck in the back of the house. George goes out through the door. He finds himself on the sundeck. It's fairly large. It has a railing around it. The sundeck and railing are made of wood. There are three patio chairs on the sundeck. There are a few towels and bathing suits hanging on the railing. The back yard is overgrown with shrubs. They look like poison ivy to George. There's no one on the sundeck or in the back yard. George walks around the sundeck. He doesn't know what to do. The sun is beating down strongly onto the sundeck. George feels the sunshine on his face and arms. This is so because they're exposed. George finds the sunshine a little oppressive. The sunshine feels a little like weight. There are houses in the back of the house. They face away from the house. George concludes there must be a street running past the fronts of the houses. At one point a woman appears from behind the house directly behind Yellow Mellow. She's in her mid twenties. She's blonde. She's very pretty. She pushes a baby carriage. It's empty. The woman walks away from the other house. She gets in between the shrubs. She proceeds walking through them. George concludes there must be a path among the shrubs. He concludes he merely can't see it. He's interested in the woman. He decides he'd like to get to know her if he'll take a share in the house. This is so in spite of her seeming to be married because of the baby carriage. George assumes he'll take a share in the house. He speaks to the woman. He asks her if she knows where the people from the house are. The woman answers she doesn't know. She says she doesn't know the people. She does this in a fairly unfriendly way. George is disappointed by her answer and manner of speaking. He watches her disappear behind the edge of Yellow Mellow. He stays on the sundeck a few more minutes. He then goes into the house. He goes into the living room. He walks around in it again. He looks at the things. He's supposed to see a man called Howie Segal. The man is in charge of the house. At one point George is near the front door. There's an end table there. There are books on top of it. There's a sheet of paper lying on top of them. George sees the sheet. There's writing on it. George reads the writing. It says:

Angie and Bill,
I am at the Pewter Tankard.
Be back late tonight.

You know where everything is. Make
yourself comfortable. See you later,

Howie

George feels relieved. He assumes the Pewter Tankard is a restaurant or bar. He decides to go there to see Howie. George walks out onto the porch. He looks to his right. The street is empty. George looks to his left. The street is also empty there. It ends about two hundred feet away. There's a fence at the end of the street. There's a hedge behind the fence. Both of these are tall. There's a building behind the hedge. There's a sign on top of the building. The sign consists of free-standing letters. It faces away from George. He reads it. It says "PEWTER TANKARD." George feels happy. There's a flag pole on top of the roof of the restaurant. There's a flag on the pole. The flag is a blue peter. It blows in the wind. The sight of the flag makes George feel happier. He doesn't know the meaning of the flag however. He decides to go to the restaurant. He gets off the porch. He turns left. He walks toward the restaurant. He assumes there's a way of getting to it from the street. Soon he sees however this isn't so. He's concerned. He turns around. He ponders. He notices two women standing in the street a few houses down. They're young. One of them is Oriental. She looks Japanese to George. He comes up to the women. He asks them how to get to the restaurant. The Oriental woman answers him. She speaks without any accent. She tells George to cross over to the street on the right. She says George can do this by turning right a few houses down. He thanks her. He follows her instructions. The next street is beyond the row of houses behind Yellow Mellow. The street is the last street in the settlement. There are dunes beyond this street. It's unpaved. It's covered with sand. The sand is deep. George has difficulty walking along the street. This is due to the sand moving under his feet. The street is sheltered. The sunshine is very hot. George gets hot. He sweats. It takes him about ten minutes to get to the restaurant. It's on the sound. There are tables outside the restaurant. Most of them are occupied. George stops. He looks at the people at the tables. He realizes he can't find Howie. This is due to George's not having seen Howie or Howie's picture before. There are waiters among the tables. The waiters run in and out of the restaurant. George plans to ask one of the waiters for Howie. They're very busy however. George walks into the restaurant. There's a bar there. There are also tables. Only a few of them are occupied. There are also only a few customers at the bar. George had expected to find pewter tankards displayed at the restaurant. There aren't any however. The shelves on the wall behind the bar are taken up with bottles. George walks up to the bar. He stands there. There are two men behind the bar. One of them comes up to George. George says he's looking for Howie Segal. George asks if the man has seen Howie. The man says he knows Howie. The man says he hasn't seen him that day however. George asks the man if the man is sure. The man answers he is. George is puzzled. He tells the man he's seen a note from Howie saying he's at the Pewter Tankard. The man says Howie works as a waiter at the restaurant. The man says Howie works in the evening. The man says he's sure Howie hasn't been at the restaurant that day. George still feels puzzled. He thanks the man for the information however. George walks out of the bar. He walks back to the house. He finds the walking even more laborious than before. He feels as if he were crippled by polio. He also feels as if he were dragging the whole world with him. On coming out onto the street with Yellow Mellow on it he stops. He looks in the direction of the house. He ponders what to do. He decides to look at the sea. He turns right. He walks to the sea. The sea is only about fifty yards beyond the dunes. There's a house immediately beyond the dunes. It's on stilts. It's propped up with beams in places. George suspects the sand had been washed out from under it. He's right in his supposition. The house is dark red. It makes George think of blood. The sea is fairly calm. It's blue. The tide is in. The beach is fairly narrow. There are quite a few people on the beach. There are steps leading down from the street to the beach. George stands at the top of the steps. He looks at the sea and beach. He does this for a few minutes. He's disappointed in the beach being narrow. He decides to go back to Yellow Mellow. He turns around. He goes to Yellow Mellow. He enters without knocking. He hears someone in the kitchen. He says hello. The person comes into the living room. It's a girl. She's in her twenties. She's of medium height and build. Her hair is of medium length. The hair is frizzy. It's brown. The girls looks Jewish. George says he's come to see if he'd like to take a share in the house. He says he wants to see Howie Segal. The girl says she can't make any arrangements. She says George should see Howie. She says Howie is on the beach. George says he's just been there. He asks where Howie is. The girl says Howie is about a hundred feet to the left of the steps leading down to the beach. She says he's with three girls. She says she's just come back from there herself. George is pleased by the news. He's excited. He says he'll go over to see Howie. George says good-bye to the girl. He says he's leaving his suitcase. He does this pointing at the suitcase. The girl says it's all right. George leaves the house. He walks to the beach. He walks fast. He nearly runs at times. He comes to the steps. He stops. He looks left. He's worried there'd be more than one man with three girls about a hundred feet to the left of the steps. George is worried he won't be able to recognize the group. About a hundred feet away to the left of the steps he sees only one man. The man is lying with five girls however. George is puzzled by this. He decides to go up to the man anyway. George goes up to the man. The man is in his early twenties. He's slightly above average in height. He's a little overweight. His hair is a little curly. It's dark brown. It's long. It reaches to below the man's shoulders. It's held together by a rubber band in the back. The hair is held in a pony tail. The man's face is attractive. The man is deeply tanned. He smiles a lot. His teeth are very white. The man reminds George of himself at the same age. George therefore likes the man from the beginning. George asks the man if the man is Howie Segal. The man answers in the affirmative. George says he'd spoken on the phone with Michael Astrakhanoff. George says he's reserved a place at the house for the weekend. He says he's interested in taking a share in the house for the summer. Howie smiles listening to George. Howie says everything is all right. He says George can stay in the house. Howie says for George to make himself comfortable. George feels relaxed. He's been squatting in front of Howie. George sits down on the sand.

6. *THE GIRLS*

Three of the girls lying with Howie are staying at Yellow Mellow. The other two are friends of the three girls. The other two girls are staying at another house. The other two girls aren't actually lying with Howie and the three girls. The other two girls lie a little farther away. Howie introduces George to the girls. The three girls staying at Yellow Mellow are Angela Pagliano, Sue McGuire, and Reina Keller. The first two girls are in their early twenties. The third girl is in her late twenties. Angela Pagliano is a dental technician. One of the aspects of her work is teaching oral hygiene. She likes her work very much. Sue McGuire is unemployed. She used to be a secretary. She wants to collect unemployment for a while. Reina Keller is a secretary. Of the three girls Angela is the most attractive. She's attractive in the stereotyped Italian way. She's fairly short. She's well-built. Her hair is black. Her eyes are brown. Angela is very tanned. She wears a brown bathing suit. Her skin is almost the same color as the bathing suit. As a result Angela seems naked at times. George likes her the most of the three girls. Almost immediately on being introduced to her he begins fantasizing about having an affair with her. This consists of how he'd spend his time with her. Part of this consists of his thinking about going abroad with her. She's called Angie by everyone. George assumes she's the Angie in the message left by Howie. George speaks about the message to Howie. George speaks about his going to the Pewter Tankard. Howie tells George the Angie in the message is someone else. Howie says the people in the message are friends of his. He says they were at the house about a month ago. He says the message dates from then. George recalls the message looking old. He finds the occurrence interesting. He finds this to be an example of how different life is from one's imagining it to be.

7. *THE FIRST RUN*

George talks to Howie and the girls. George is wearing swimming trunks under his clothes. He takes off his clothes after about ten minutes. He lies down on the sand. It gets to be about four. George finds this out by looking at his watch. He's a long-distance runner. He runs every day. He usually runs in the morning. He hasn't run yet that day. He decides to take a run. He asks the people if they'll stay on the beach for another hour. They answer in the affirmative. George asks them to watch over his clothes. He says he'll take a run. He runs between nine and twenty miles every day. He mentions how much he runs. Everyone's amazed. George is pleased by it. He's wearing a wrist watch. It's a stop watch. George says good-bye to the people. He starts the watch. Simultaneously with this he starts running. He runs east. He starts out fast. This is so in order to impress Howie and the girls. George then slows down a little. After warming up he runs fast again. He runs faster than at the beginning. He feels good. He feels as though flying. His feet seem to be wings. This impression is heightened by the shape of human feet. The shape of human feet makes George think of the wings of such birds as eagles, hawks, and crows. This is due to the feathers of these birds being spread on the ends of the wings like toes. There's a west wind. George feels it on his back. The wind seems to be pushing him along quite strongly. His torso seems to be filled by it. It's as if the torso were a sail. The sky is still blue. George sees it. It makes him think he's a blue sail. There's a settlement less than a mile along the beach in that direction. Many of the houses are very close to the beach. They're fairly far apart. They're all very large. They're obviously old. They date probably from the twenties. The houses make George think of high society in the twenties at Newport, R.I. Most of the houses are architecturally interesting. They all have their roofs and walls covered by shingles. This imparts elegance to the houses. The spacing between and the size of the houses remind George of whales or specters. George likes the similarity. He's planning to run as far as Cherry Grove. He thinks Fire Island Pines is west of Cherry Grove. It's the other way around. George therefore will run to Fire Island Pines. He passes more settlements before coming to Cherry Grove. They aren't visible from the beach however. George is aware of them due to the concentration of the people on the beach. The settlements George has been passing are heterosexual. The sexual composition of the people on the beach is about equally male and female. The two sexes are mixed about equally. George comes to Cherry Grove. The people there on the beach are mostly men. George notices this. He assumes the settlement is Fire Island Pines. As was mentioned, this isn't so. The men are mostly in couples. Many of the men walk. This is much more common than on the heterosexual beaches. The ratio of women to men on the beach is less than one to ten. Most of the women are together. Most of the women are also in couples. Most of these couples also walk. Many of the women look like men. This contrasts with the men. Very few of them look like women. The sight of the couples brings out resentment in George. This is about equally true of the male and female couples. The resentment is due to a recent experience in George's life. At one point George passes a group of Japanese people. There are four of them. They are a man, woman, boy, and girl. The boy and girl look about eight and seven respectively. George is surprised by the sight of the family. He wonders if the people came to the settlement without being aware of its being homosexual. George feels this could be due to the people's being foreigners. Shortly after passing the Japanese family he passes a man. The man is dressed in a shirt, pants, and shoes. He looks in his fifties. He's tall. He doesn't look homosexual. He's walking along the beach. He's walking toward George. On George's reaching the man the latter asks George what time it is. George stops. He stops the watch. He looks at it. He tells the man the time. The man thanks George. George tells the man he's welcome. The man resumes walking in his original direction. George starts the watch. He simultaneously starts running. He realizes he'd been glad to tell the man the time. George realizes he's pleased to have been stopped by the man. George realizes he'd found the man pleasant. George is a little upset about this. This is due to there being a good chance of the man's being homosexual. George forces himself to stop thinking about this however. He feels there's a good chance of there being no reason for his worrying about this. He tries to recapture his previous feeling derived from running. He succeeds in this fairly soon. From remembering the time he'd told the man George estimates he has another three quarters of a mile to run to cover the desired distance. George estimates the spot on the beach where this'd be. He decides to run there.

8. *FUNERAL PROCESSION*

George runs on. He passes Cherry Grove. He comes to Fire Island Pines. He sees flags and decorations on some of the houses. He thinks the settlement looks nice. He used to run to this settlement from the opposite direction. He recognizes some of the buildings. He used to think this was Cherry Grove. This is the reason for his thinking Cherry Grove is Fire Island Pines. George comes to the spot he'd planned to run to. This is at the eastern end of Fire Island Pines. George turns around. He continues running at the same pace. Within less than a quarter of a mile he comes across the following procession. The procession walks along the beach. The procession walks toward George. It consists of seven men. Five of them look normal. They're white. They're dressed in normal clothes. The clothes consist of sports shirts and sports pants or bathing suits. One of the other men is also white. He looks in his twenties. He looks Italian. His hair is fairly long. It's curly. It looks like a woman's. The man's face is very pretty. It also looks like a woman's. The man is about five feet ten. He's slender. He's wearing earrings. They're gold. The man is also wearing a bracelet on his left wrist. The bracelet is also gold. The man is wearing eye makeup and lipstick. He's dressed in a shirt and pants. The shirt has long sleeves. They're full. The shirt is made from a sheer fabric. The shirt is white. The pants are tight. They're also white. The man doesn't seem to be wearing underpants. He swings his arms in an exaggerated fashion. His wrists are limp. The movement of his hands therefore is very exaggerated. The man swings his hips while walking. His eyes are partly raised. The man seemed to be looking at the sky. He doesn't seem to be seeing anything near by. There's an expression of distress on his face. The distress is obviously faked. It's overdone. It's like that of an actress in a silent movie. The other man is black. He looks in his late twenties. He's about five feet eight. He's well built. He's not exceptionally well built however. He's wearing a caveman's bathing suit. It has a strap going over the left shoulder. The suit is spotted like a leopard's skin. The background of the suit is green. The spots are yellow. The black man is walking on the other man's right side. The black man has his left arm around the other man's waist. The black man's body isn't pressed to the other man's body however. This permits the other man to walk as described. The black man has a very proud expression on his face. He's obviously very pleased to be in the company of the other man. The black man looks most of the time at the other man. The other five men walk behind the two men. The other five men walk a few steps behind the two men. The other five men aren't looking in any special way at the two men. The other five men don't talk however. This seems to imply they're at least pleased to be in the company of the two men. George sees the procession. He can't believe his eyes. He's ashamed to look at the procession. He's afraid this'd indicate he finds it outrageous. He can't keep himself from looking at it completely however. He looks at it a total of five times. During this time he manages to form a picture of the procession as described above. He passes the procession. He runs on. He can't get rid of the image of the procession for the rest of the run.

9. *SUPPER*

George had been to a summer house before. In that house supper was fixed for everyone. George was assuming this'd be true in this house. This isn't so however. Howie is out working at the Pewter Tankard. The four girls fix supper for themselves. There's no store in Robin's Rest for George to buy something to eat. He doesn't feel like going to the Pewter Tankard alone. He stays around the house. The girls offer him some food. Reina is a vegetarian. She made a vegetable stew. Angela warmed up a can of spaghetti and meatballs. Sue made some boiled chicken. Risa is eating with Reina. Each girl gives George left-over food. In addition there's some bread in the house. The girls tell George he can have some bread. He eats the food. He feels a little ashamed accepting it. On the other hand he's pleased by both being offered the food and accepting it. He feels it befits his situation. It's as if he considered himself a beggar. He's not conscious of these emotions. Angela has eaten already. Sue eats in the living room. Reina and Risa eat at the dining-room table. George eats with Reina and Risa. He eats after the two girls have eaten about half of their food. This is when he's offered the food by them. There's a strong sunlight coming in through the dining-room window. This is so even though the sun is quite low. Actually, it's due to this. This is so because of the sunlight reaching into the dining room because of being low. The sun is shining in George's eyes. He can hardly see the food.

10. *PARTS OF TWO LIFE STORIES*

Reina is Jewish. She's sephardic. Her maiden name is Toledano. Reina is twenty-eight years old. She's divorced. Her husband's name was George. The couple were married three years. Reina didn't suspect any trouble. The couple were in the process of buying a house. One day they were going to have guests for supper. Reina and her husband had talked about the affair the night before. She wasn't feeling well that day. In addition to that she had a lot of cooking to do. As a consequence she came home from work early. The husband's car was parked in front of the apartment house. There were his things in the car. Reina had a premonition something bad was happening. She walked into the building. Her heart was beating loudly. She met her husband in the lobby. He was carrying his suits on hangers. He wasn't embarrassed to see Reina. He told her he'd had it. He said he didn't want to be married to her any longer. Reina asked him why he hadn't indicated there was a problem earlier. He answered why should it matter. He said he wanted out of the marriage now. He said this was what mattered. He moved in with a girl. Reina got divorced a year later. She's undergoing psychiartic treatment. It consists of psychotherapy. Risa is twenty-five years old. She's a psychiatric therapist. She's also Jewish. She works at a mental hospital. It's a state hospital. Risa likes her profession. She doesn't like her job. This is due to the personalities of some of her co-workers. Risa is an only child. She lives with her parents. Her mother is a very strong person psychologically. Risa describes her mother as a bull. Risa's father is docile. Risa has psychological problems. She's neurotic and borderline schizophrenic. She's undergoing psychiatric treatment. It consists of psychoanalysis and chemotherapy.

11. *AT THE PEWTER TANKARD*

After supper George goes to the Pewter Tankard. He goes there with Angela and Sue. They stay at the bar. They drink. George stays near Angela. He talks almost exclusively with her. He doesn't find Sue attractive. George and Angela talk about rock music. He likes rock music very much. He listens to hardly any other kind of music. This is so in spite of his having listened only to classical music at one time. George is trying to convince Angela of his really liking rock music. This is so in order to appear younger in her eyes. George does this by talking about different rock groups, their albums and songs. The radio is on in the bar. At one point Elton John's "Honky Cat" comes on. George, Angela and Sue immediately start moving to the music. Angela says she wants to test George if he really knows rock music. She asks him to identify the song. He laughs. He finds the test very easy. He gives Angela the information. She replies he's right. He has an unpleasant feeling about the test. He doesn't know why. He doesn't try finding this out however. He tries suppressing the feeling. He has trouble doing this. In the end he's no longer conscious of the feeling. The feeling stays in his subconscious however. At one point George has to urinate. He goes to the toilet. The urinal there is very high up on the wall. The urinal is almost too high for George to use. This is so in spite of his not being short. The washbasin on the other hand is unusually low. The washbasin is lower than the urinal. It's as if the washbasin and the urinal were reversed. It's as if this'd been done as a joke.

12. *NIGHT ON THE TOWN*

George, Angela, and Sue go to Ocean Beach. They'll go barhopping there. They'll try picking up someone. Reina and Risa have already gone there straight from the house. Howie has gone to work at the Pewter Tankard. Howie had gotten dressed up. He'd put his hair up in a pony tail. He'd put a rubber band around his hair. He'd stuffed the pony tail down his shirt collar in the back. This way he seems to have short hair. The management at the restaurant had told him to do this. It's dark. The moon is shining. George and the girls walk along the path among the reeds. There's no one around. The moonlight illuminates the road and the reeds. It seems daytime. Objects aren't as clear however as in the daytime. It's as if the world were an underexposed photograph. George is Ukrainian. He was born and raised in the Ukraine. He's reminded of some scenes from the life of Zaporozhian Cossacks he'd seen in books in his childhood. This is so because of the reeds and the moonlight. Zaporozhian Cossacks lived on islands in the Dnieper river. There were many reeds there. Zaporozhian Cossacks' campaigns were conducted frequently at night. George remembers his childhood. He felt happy then. He's forgotten about it. He's forgotten what happiness is. It seems incongruous to him to have felt happy at one time. The memory of his happiness serves as a relief for him. He and the girls walk into Ocean Beach. The streets are lit. George and the girls pass the church George had passed on the way from the boat. The church is illuminated by spotlights. It's white against the sky. This is so in spite of the sky being relatively light. The church reminds George of New England. Specifically, the church reminds him of Paul Revere's ride. This is so because of George's having seen a picture of Paul Revere riding past a white church. There are people in the streets. The people aren't numerous however. The atmosphere is strangely hushed. It seems to be the eve before a big holiday. The hushed atmosphere is primarily due to there being no vehicular traffic. The girls have a particular bar in mind. George and they go there. There are many people in the bar. There's a juke box there. It's playing. The music is rock. The bar has a dance floor. The dance floor is next to the bar. There are people dancing there. There are many of them. The dance floor is packed with people. It's almost impossible to dance. George and the girls head for the bar. They stand at the bar. They wait to be served. The bartender waits on them. George and the girls order their drinks. George and the girls wait for the drinks. The drinks come. George and the girls drink. George looks around. He thinks he should ask Angela to dance. He's reluctant to do this because of being much older than she. He forces himself to do this. Angela agrees to dance. George and Angela dance. They dance in place. This is due to it being very crowded. George and Angela move provocatively while dancing. At one point she tells him he dances well. She seems surprised. George is pleased by this. He smiles. He feels hopeful about having success with Angela. The music stops. George and Angela go back to the bar. Sue is still there. She's still drinking. George and Angela continue finishing their drinks. The music starts again. George thinks he should wait asking Angela to dance again. He thinks he should wait until the next song. Sue is sitting on a stool. At one point one of the stools next to her is vacated. Angela sits down on this stool. She faces the bar. She and Sue talk. They seem to have forgotten George. He feels a little left out. He tries to supress the feeling. He thinks he's too sensitive. He turns away from the girls. He looks at the people dancing. Many of them are his age or older. Most of them are overweight. The people's bodies quiver during the people's dancing. The sight is unpleasant. George feels a revulsion at the sight. He feels contempt for the people. This turns into contempt for people in general. George includes himself among the people. He feels depressed. At one point he turns back to the bar. Angela is no longer sitting at it. She's next to her stool. She's dancing. Opposite her is a man. He's young. He's in his early twenties. He looks a hippy. He's very thin. He's very ugly. He's dancing too. He's obviously dancing with Angela. At one point George catches a glimpse of her face. It's radiant. George hasn't seen her face like this. He realizes she's very happy dancing with the man. George remembers her face during her dancing with him. He realizes she'd been bored then. He feels gloomy in an instant because of that. He turns away from the couple. He looks at the crowd again. He finds the sight of the crowd less unpleasant than that of the couple. The feeling of revulsion continues in him however. He finishes his drink. He continues standing in the same position. He holds his glass. He clutches it. His fingers grow white from the pressure. At one point his eyes wander off from the crowd. They focus on a table beyond the dance area. The table is close to the door. A girl sits there. She looks drunk. She's alone at the table. She's leaning her head on her hand. Her hair is obscuring her face. The hair is frizzy. It's brown. George realizes the girl is Risa. He cheers up. It's Risa's appearance that cheers him up. He turns around. He puts his glass on the bar. He pays no attention to Angela and her dancing partner. George wends his way past the dancing couples. He goes to Risa's table. He stops at it. He puts his hand on Risa's shoulder. He shakes Risa gently. He asks her what's wrong. Risa looks up. She looks very gloomy. She says hello. There's no chair next to the table. George sits down on top of the table. He and Risa talk. She tells him what'd happened. She's in love with a man. He's twenty. He plays in a band. It's performing in one of the bars. Risa has been there. The man had paid no attention to her. She got drunk because of that. She hates herself for being in love with the man. She can't kill her love however. George feels the situation might be right for his seducing Risa. He talks to her. He tries convincing her she should forget the man. George says she's too intelligent and mature for the man. By mature George means old. He asks Risa to go back to the house with him. He says they can sit and talk. He says he can help her. She doesn't agree to this however. She says she'll stay on in town. She says she has to talk to the man that night. She says she wants to find out if he does love her even a little. George goes on trying to convince Risa to go with him. He feels bad about this. He feels humiliated. He feels as if begging for alms. Part of his feeling comes from the fact Risa isn't attractive. To George this is an indication of how low he's sunk. At one point Risa seems more interested in him than until then. She listens to him talk. She apparently finds something attractive about him. She asks him how old he is. He decides to lie. He says he's thirty-seven. He's thirty-nine. Risa seems to believe him. She doesn't say anything. She hangs her head down. It's as if she found thirty-seven too old. It's as if she'd thought George is younger. He's surprised by this. He feels thirty-seven is young. He feels twelve years difference between a man and a girl isn't bad. He therefore feels there's something wrong with Risa. He feels he's not interested in someone like that. He therefore stops trying to convince Risa to go with him. He changes the subject. He says he wants to look around the town by himself. He asks what kind of bars are there around. Risa gives him a few names. She tells him a few places not to go to. She says they're frequented by teenagers only. She says even she's too old for them. George tries not to pay any attention to her warning. He feels now even more than before there's something wrong with Risa. He feels she has a strange hangup about age. He feels age doesn't matter. This is so in spite of his being uptight about his age.

13. *ALONE*

The night life in Ocean Beach is concentrated along a few streets. George walks along these streets. There are many people there. There are diners, bars, and discotheques along these streets. All of these establishements are crowded. George wants to go to a bar or a discotheque. He goes into a few of them. They're packed with people. Besides, George doesn't like the atmosphere there. He's overcome by fright on entering each of the establishments. One of them is among those he's been warned about by Risa. He tries to go into it. One has to pay an admission fee to enter the establishment. George looks inside the establishment from the door. A raucous music is playing inside. The place is packed with people. They're mostly teenagers. Most of them are dancing. The establishment is fairly brightly illuminated. The light is blue. It's unpleasant. It makes George think of a morgue. He therefore very hastily turns back from the door of the establishment. He retains an unpleasant feeling from the association with a morgue. The feeling is like an unpleasant taste. Shortly thereafter George passes a diner. It's relatively empty. George goes inside the diner. He orders a glass of orange juice. He drinks the juice. Shortly thereafter he goes back to the house. The moon is still out. On walking along the reed-surrounded portion of the path George has the same sensation as walking into town. This calms him down. He feels sleepy. He's planning to go to sleep on coming to the house. He's looking forward to this.

14. *IN BED*

George was told by Howie to use a particular room. It's large. It has three beds. They're double beds. There's no light in the room. George has to undress and make his bed in the dark. He has trouble falling asleep. It takes him about two hours to do this. Shortly after his falling asleep he's awakened by people coming back to the house. He recognizes the voices of the people. They're the girls. They come separately. They all come with men. On coming to the house Reina looks for a free room. This is due to her staying in a room with Risa. Reina walks into George's room. She apparently thinks it's empty. She sees George there. She says: "Oh, I'm sorry!" She closes the door. She walks away. Reina's tone of voice was very kind. George is surprised by it. This is due to his impression of Reina being coarse. George wasn't sure if she'd come with a man. He was hoping she wanted to spend the night with him. He's disappointed at her having walked away. This is so in spite of his not finding her attractive. George thinks her walking away might be due to his not having asked her to come in. He feels a little guilty about this. He's fairly sure however of Reina having brought a man along. George falls asleep again. At one point he's awakened by soft laughter. It's about four in the morning. The laughter is that of a girl and a man. George isn't sure of all the girls having come in before. He thinks the laughter belongs to Sue. He's not sure however. The laughter comes from under the window in his room. The window opens out onto the porch. It sounds as though the couple are planning to sleep there. George assumes this is so because of Sue's and Angela's staying in one room. He assumes Angela had arrived at the house before Sue. He assumes Angela and a man had occupied the room. The couple continue laughing and talking. George is waiting for the boards to creak. He's expecting this to happen during the couple's having intercourse. The laughter has a soothing effect on him. He falls asleep again. He never finds out whether the couple had intercourse. A little later he's awakened by the sound of rain. It's getting light outside. It's gray. The sound of the rain is similar to the previous laughter. The sound of the rain is just as soothing to George as the laughter. He falls asleep again.

15. *IN THE MORNING*

The rain has stopped by eight in the morning. George wakes up shortly thereafter. He can only hear the water dripping off the roof. The sound is like that of someone finishing whispering. It's almost as dark as during George's waking up at dawn. George decides to take his run. He decides to run in his trunks. He puts them on. He goes out into the living room. There are a man and a girl sleeping on the two couches there. George doesn't recognize the couple. He walks out onto the porch. There's no one there. George observes the couple in the living room could be the one from the porch. The sky is heavily overcast.

16. *THE SECOND RUN*

George runs along the beach. He runs in the same direction as the day before. He plans to run to the same spot as the day before. There's no one around. The tide is high. The waves aren't very big. They break high on the beach. The waves breaking look like artillery shells exploding. This makes George a little depressed. After about fifteen minutes since his staring to run it starts raining. The rain gets quite strong. George can feel the rain hitting his body. The rain feels like the fingers of a drummer on a drum skin. George likes the comparison. This makes him feel better. The comparison to a drum makes him think of being dead. This is so because of his thinking of his skin being stretched out on the drum. This doesn't detract from his liking the comparison of himself with a drum. The clouds at this point seem to have gotten lower. They seem to be travelling very fast. They're moving west. The sight of the clouds and the rain remind George of a run he'd taken along the beach on

Fire Island a little less than two years ago. It was in October. George was running with another person. It was raining as heavily as now. The clouds were just as dark and low. They were moving just as fast in the same direction. At one point George noticed birds flying. They were moving in the same direction as the clouds. The birds were moving faster however. They were flying below the clouds. The birds were flying very low. This was probably because of the wind being weaker there. The birds were flying above the water. There were many of them. The space above the water was almost packed with them. The space was black in places. The birds flew in formations. The formations seemed trains. The trains seemed freight trains. They seemed overloaded with people. The people seemed war refugees. The birds seemed war refugees. George stopped on seeing the birds. He waited for the person running with him to reach him. George pointed out the birds to the person. George found the sight extremely beautiful. He couldn't tear his eyes away from the birds. He stood still for a while. He then continued running. He continued looking at the birds. He could hardly think of anything else after that for days. He hasn't forgotten the sight of the birds.

17. *BREAKFAST*

George fixes breakfast for himself. Howie had told George George can use anything he wants in the kitchen. George has cornflakes with milk, tea with sugar, white bread with butter, and one soft-boiled egg. He feels better about everything during and after the breakfast. This is partly due to the warmth of the tea and egg. The warmth makes George feel cozy. The girls and Howie are in the house during George's having breakfast. The girls are drinking coffee, reading, and talking. Howie is in his bedroom. There's no one else in the house.

18. *TALKING*

The girls talk about the experiences of the preceding night. At one point Reina tells her story. She's angry about what'd happened. There's however a note of mirth in her voice. It therefore sounds as though Reina had enjoyed what'd happened. The name of the man who'd come with her was George. She points out the name is the same as that of her husband. She doesn't point out the name is the same as that of George. She says the man had said to her in the morning: "I gotta tell you one thing—I'm married. . . ." She laughs at this point. She says: "Goddammit, George, if you're married, tell it to me before and not after!" She laughs again.

19. *GOOD-BYE*

During the run George had decided to leave. He'd told this to Howie before having breakfast. George packs after breakfast. He brings out his suitcase into the living room. He comes up to Howie. George takes out his wallet. He'd been told by Michael the price for the weekend was thirty dollars. George takes thirty dollars out of his wallet. He gives the money to Howie. Howie looks at the money. He says George hasn't stayed the whole weekend. Howie says the weekend includes Friday night. He says, besides, George is leaving early. Howie says he'll charge George therefore only twenty dollars. Howie gives ten dollars back to George. George takes the money. He's moved by Howie's gesture. He feels sorry about leaving. He says he might come back another weekend. He says good-bye to everyone.

20. *ADVICE*

While saying good-bye to George Risa gives him advice. She says the house and Robin's Rest aren't for him. She says the people there are too young. She says George would enjoy himself more at another settlement. She says such a settlement is Kismet. She says there are many divorced people there. She says they're of George's age. George doesn't fail to observe the settlement is the one the dumpy woman was going to.

21. *RETREAT*

It's raining during George's going back to the boat. The rain is light however. The suitcase seems heavier to George than the day before.

He carries the suitcase in his right hand. He's wearing shorts as when he arrived. The suitcase is rubbing against the outside of his right leg. There's a tear in the side of the suitcase. The tear is on the side rubbing George's leg. The edges of the tear are sharp. They scrape against George's leg. George finds the sensation unpleasant. He carried the suitcase turned the other way when he arrived. He doesn't feel like turning the suitcase around now. He feels it'd be too much trouble. Walking along the part of the path surrounded by reeds, he remembers the sensation evoked in him by them the previous night. He can't recapture the sensation. It's as if he didn't know what it is. It's as if someone had merely told him about it. It's as if George had never had this sensation. Going to the boat terminal he takes a street he'd walked along the night before. This is the street with the luncheonette and the teenager discotheque on it. The street doesn't look as depressing to George as the night before. He remembers however the sensation he'd had there.

22. *ON THE BOAT*

The boat is packed with people. This is undoubtedly due to the rain. Many of the people are leaving because of there not being anything to do on the island in the rain. It's actually the covered portion of the boat that's packed with people. This is also due to the rain. People don't want to get wet. George couldn't get a seat. He's standing. He's in the center of the boat. The suitcase is between his legs. There are bars overhead. There are life vests stacked on top of the bar. George is holding onto one of the bars. The sea is choppy. The boat is rocking. George therefore has to hold onto the bar pretty strongly. This is especially so when the boat lurches vertically or horizontally. George looks at his hand. It's white. George's wrist is broad. It's also white. Because of the pressure the hand is distorted. The hand at times doesn't look to George like a hand. It looks then to him like the base of a tree. The tree seems big. It seems strong. George seems to be growing into the bar through his hand. He's pleased by this. He's pleased at his hand looking so organic and strong. Five of the people next to him are friends of each other. They're middle-aged. They seem Jewish. Three of them are men. Two are women. Two of the men seem married to the women. The people talk. The man seeming unmarried talks the most. He seems to have gotten divorced not very long ago. The time could be between a year and three years.

The man seems not to have seen the people since his divorce. He seems to have just come across them. He tells them how well he's doing since getting divorced. He speaks of his professional success. He does this without mentioning the nature of his profession. He also says he's playing tennis. He says he's better now than ever. He says he's jogging. He says he jogs about two miles a day. He says he couldn't run a quarter of a mile at the beginning. He says he stuck with it. He says he'd jog a quarter. He says he'd then walk a quarter. He says he'd then jog again. He says he was thus able to progress to running the full two miles. The other four people express admiration for the man. They do this usually through asking questions. The questions imply admiration. George is listening to the people for a while. With time he gets bored with the conversation. His attention wanders off. The man has a booming voice. The engine makes a deep sound. The sound is similar to the man's voice. With time the two sounds merge in George's mind. They begin to sound to George like his own heartbeat. He's standing close to the window. At this point he's looking outside. He's doing this absentmindedly. The spray is hitting the window. The spray is flowing down the window. The spray is almost completely covering the window. The spray is refracting the light coming in from the outside. The world looks white.

ELEANOR

Eleanor is thirty-four. She's very beautiful. She's five feet three inches tall. She weighs ninety-two pounds. Her hair is very thick. It's wavy. It doesn't quite reach to the shoulders. It's golden. It has a reddish tinge. The hair is parted down the middle of the head. The hair is a little darker at the roots seen along the part than further out. This isn't because of the hair being dyed however. It's straight at the roots. It gets wavier toward the ends. Eleanor's complexion is very smooth. It's fair. It seems Eleanor is wearing makeup. This isn't true however. Eleanor's eyebrows are very thin. They seem plucked. They seem painted. These facts also aren't true however. The eyebrows are reddish-brown. Eleanor's eyes are large. They're oval. They're brown. Eleanor's nose is straight. It's of medium length and width. Eleanor's lips are full. They're red. They aren't painted however. Eleanor's chin is delicate. It's a little recessed. This doesn't detract from Eleanor's beauty however. On the contrary, it makes Eleanor more beautiful. It makes her seem fragile. This makes her seem more feminine. This finally makes her seem more beautiful. Her neck is thin. It looks strong however. Eleanor's bust is small. Her wrists, hands, and feet are fine. Eleanor wears a blouse, bracelet, belt, skirt and petticoat. The blouse has no collar. The blouse has a wide neck. The neck is quite low. The blouse is loose at the bust. The blouse has long sleeves. They're full. They're gathered at the shoulders. The sleeves are embroidered just below the shoulders. The embroidery doesn't quite reach to the elbows. It's floral. It's represented in horizontal lines. They're wavy. They look like sea waves. This gives the blouse the appearance of the sea.

The blouse looks even more like the sea because of the sleeves being full. The blouse looks like the sea at high tide. The sleeves are open at the ends. The sleeves are also wide at the ends. The sleeves don't quite reach to the wrists. The blouse is made from a thin material. The material is cotton. It seems handwoven. It's dark blue. This makes the blouse look still more like the sea. The embroidery is dark red. The blouse seems to have been made in an underdeveloped country. The country seems one of the Eastern countries. It could be one of the Arab countries, Iran, Afghanistan, or India for instance. The bracelet is a string of beads. They're fairly small. They're clay. They're glazed. They're dark green. Eleanor wears the bracelet on her left wrist. The string is wrapped four times around the wrist. The belt is about three inches wide. It's about five feet long. It's cloth. It has a fringe at its ends. The belt has a pattern. The pattern is geometric. It's very delicate. The belt is mostly red. The red is paler than that of the embroidery in the blouse. The pattern is black and white. The belt is handmade. It was made in the Ukraine. The belt is wrapped twice around Eleanor's waist. The ends of the belt hang loose. Each of them is on the outside of one of Eleanor's hips. The skirt is full. It's long. It doesn't quite reach to Eleanor's ankles. It's made from a thin material. The material is cotton. It has a hound's-tooth pattern. The pattern is quite fine. It's pale blue and white. The skirt was made by a friend of Eleanor's. The friend is a girl. She was sixteen at the time. She lives now in Arizona. The petticoat is slightly longer than the skirt. The petticoat is made from linen. The linen is fairly coarse. It's natural color. The color is ivory. The linen seems handwoven. The petticoat is embroidered at the bottom. The embroidery is also floral. The flowers are different however than those on the blouse. They're red. The red is a little lighter than that of the embroidery on the blouse. The red is a little darker than that of the belt. The stems are blue. The blue of the stems is also lighter than that of the blouse. The blue of the stems is darker however than the blue of the skirt. The petticoat seems handmade. Eleanor could have made it herself. She's barefoot. She's come over this way. She's walked all the way from her home. The distance is close to two miles. Eleanor's feet are surprisingly clean however. They're dirty only on the bottoms. The dirty part constitutes a well-defined shape. It's very delicate. It's very thin in the metatarsal part of the foot for instance. The width of the dirty part in that area is about half an inch. The dirty part is smooth. It shines. It's black. It seems a piece of leather attached to the bottom of Eleanor's foot. The leather seems to be sewn on. This is so in spite of there being no trace of stitches. Eleanor is divorced. She's been divorced for three years. She'd been separated from her husband for five years prior to becoming divorced. She'd lived with her husband three years prior to becoming separated. Her husband was a mulatto. Eleanor has two children from the marriage. They're a boy and a girl. They're ten and nine years old respectively. The boy looks Negroid. He's ugly. He's not ugly because of looking Negroid however. He seems an imbecile. He's normal however. The girl looks nearly Caucasian. She's pretty. Eleanor used to be a fashion model. She used to be a very good fashion model. She used to be one of the top two or three fashion models in the country. She has given up her profession however. She did this because of not believing in her work. She found the work dishonest. This was so because of modeling being a part of advertising. This was in turn so because of advertising being such a powerful tool of capitalism. Eleanor quit her profession in the following way. She felt very guilty at being a model. This constituted a psychological stress for her. As a consequence she developed a severe case of peritonitis. Her life was in danger. Eleanor pulled out of this however. But her health is very poor now. Eleanor has chronic peritonitis. This manifests itself in her getting an infection every one or two months. Her glands then become swollen and painful. Eleanor also gets eruptions on her body. One place she gets them is on her left ring finger. These eruptions look like blisters. The eruptions appear anywhere on the finger from its tip to the base. They come in a cluster. It's the size of a large pea. The eruptions are painful. Eleanor used to take antibiotics for peritonitis. She's stopped doing this however. This was so because of her noticing deteriorations in her skin due to the antibiotics. She was afraid of how her internal organs might be affected by the antibiotics. Her internal organs have definitely been affected by the peritonitis. This includes her reproductive organs. Eleanor is now very weak physically. She'll be like this for the rest of her life. As a matter of fact she'll be getting progressively worse. A little more of her body is damaged with each attack of the peritonitis. Eleanor works as a makeup artist. She works only about four days a month. She makes this way enough money to support herself and her children. She likes her work. One reason for this is her being able to sit down at her job. This is so because of her aforementioned physical weakness. Eleanor lives with two friends. They're a man and a woman. They live together. The woman is the wife of a writer friend of Eleanor's. The woman and the writer friend are separated. They'll probably get divorced soon. Eleanor lives with the people because of not being able to afford a place of her own. She's planning to work straight through for about two weeks this time. This is so because of her wanting to save up some money. She's planning to use the money to go to Arizona. She's planning to stay there with her aforementioned friend. Eleanor used to be a very heavy drug taker. She took drugs like grass, hash, acid, coke, etc. The two common drugs she hasn't taken are heroin and speed. She's planning to take speed some day however. She's planning to take speed once or twice. She's planning to take speed so few times because of feeling speed is dangerous. She feels this is especially so for her because of her physical condition. She however wants to take speed because of the effect of speed. She feels speed brings out a person's ultimate physical capabilities. She takes now only grass, hash, and coke. She's given up acid because of its destructive effect on a person's neural system. Eleanor doesn't feel the drugs she's taking now are detrimental to her health. She also doesn't feel her peritonitis had been at least partly brought on by her being a heavy drug user. This is possibly true however. Eleanor is a disciple of occultism. This has changed her personality completely. She's very calm. She's non-violent. She's a vegetarian. She also never judges people. She's against technology. She uses only natural things. At this moment she's sitting in a chair. The chair has arm rests. Its seat is round. The chair is wicker. It has a cushion on it. The cushion fits the seat of the chair. The cushion is plastic. It's stuffed with foam rubber. The rubber is in one piece. The plastic is bright red. The red of the plastic is paler than any of the reds mentioned so far. Eleanor is sitting at a table. It's fairly large. It's round. It has one leg. The table is wooden. It's covered with a piece of cloth. The cloth is fairly thick. It's wool. It has a pattern in it. The pattern is geometric. The pattern in the cloth is different from that in Eleanor's belt however. The pattern in the cloth consists of thin parallel lines. They're fairly widely spaced. The cloth is red. The red of the cloth is lighter than that of the embroidery on the petticoat. The red of the cloth is darker however than that of the belt. The cloth was handwoven. It was made in Morocco. Eleanor has been speaking with George. He sits in the same kind of chair as she. He also sits at the table. He's facing Eleanor. He's a writer. He says he'd like Eleanor to read a particular thing of his. She agrees to the suggestion. George gets up from the chair. He walks out of the room. He goes into the hallway. He crosses it. He goes into one of the rooms off the hallway. There's a suitcase lying on the floor in that room. The suitcase is of the folding type. The suitcase is made from a thin material. The material is plastic. It's gray. The suitcase is laid out flat. There's a flap on the inside of the suitcase. The flap has a zipper running along its three sides. The flap is unzipped. The flap is closed however. George goes up to the suitcase. He squats down. He throws back the flap. The suitcase is full of clothes. They're neatly folded. There's a folder lying on top of them. The folder is paper. It's dark red. The red of the folder is about like that of the embroidery in the blouse. George picks up the folder. He opens it. There's a writing pad in the folder. The pad is quadrille. It's white. The top page of the pad is covered with writing. The writing is practically illegible. It was written with a ball-point pen. The tip of the pen was fine. The ink is blue. The blue is about the same as that of the skirt. There are pockets on each side of the inside of the folder. They have pages stuck in them. The pages are typewritten. George flips the writing pad over to the left. The top five pages in the right pocket are stapled together. They're Xeroxed. They constitute what George wants Eleanor to read. He's been through a traumatic experience recently. The pages constitute a description of the experience. The description is written in prose. The description is poetry however. George takes the stapled pages out of the pocket. He closes the folder. He puts it in its original place. He closes the flap. He stands up. He goes to the room he's come from. He goes to the table. He hands the pages to Eleanor. She takes them. George sits down in his chair. He looks at Eleanor. The first paragraph takes up about two thirds of the page. The paragraph speaks of George's heart tolling like a bell all afternoon. The bell seems to toll for George. He's been away most of the day. He arrives home. His second car is missing. George tries to visualize the car as if to catch his breath. All the windows in the house are wide open. George can't distinguish between his chest and the house. The windows therefore seem to be open in his chest. His chest therefore seems very empty. George goes into the house. He goes to the kitchen. There's a letter lying on the kitchen counter. The letter is typewritten. It's written on a white sheet of paper. George picks up the letter. He reads it. He holds the sheet in both his hands. They're steady. The sheet however seems to move. It's like a hand waving good-bye. It seems to be waving good-bye to George. He finishes the letter. He's very upset. He tries to calm himself down. He strokes his body with his hand. This doesn't help however. George goes to look for his guns. They're missing. They seem to be missing like children. The children seem George's. George calls out to his guns. They don't appear. There's a garden behind the house. George runs out into the garden. He calls out to his guns again. He waits. There's no answer. Eleanor reads to the end of the paragraph. She likes the writing very much. She then stops. She feels she's read enough. She feels she's grasped George's intent. She feels no need to read on. She tells George her opinion of the paragraph. Her face was calm before. It's now even calmer. Eleanor's lips are a little distended. A smile seems about to form itself on them. The lips are like the part of the horizon from behind which the sun is about to rise. The smile seems the sun. Eleanor puts the pages down on the table. She gets up from the chair. There's a sofa in the room. The sofa is quite long. It has a high back and sides. The back and sides are of the same height. The sofa is old-fashioned. It's been recently upholstered. It's been upholstered with a thin material. The material is cotton. It has a pattern. The pattern is also floral. The flowers in the material however are neither like those in Eleanor's blouse nor petticoat. The flowers in the material are of the type used in Indian fabrics. The background of the material is beige. The flowers are red, blue, and green. The red and blue are very much like those of the embroidery on Eleanor's petticoat. The green is paler than that of Eleanor's bracelet however. There's a cushion on the sofa. The cushion is large. It's square. It's filled with foam rubber. The rubber is cut up into small pieces. The cushion is covered with a fairly thick material. The material also has a pattern. The pattern is also floral. The flowers in the cushion are unlike any of those mentioned so far however. The flowers in the cushion are quite realistic. They're quite large. The background of the material is dark blue. The blue of the cushion is paler than that of Eleanor's blouse. The blue of the cushion is darker than that of the embroidery on Eleanor's petticoat however. The blue of the cushion is impure. The flowers are green and yellow. The green is darker than the green of Eleanor's bracelet. There's a light in the middle of the ceiling. The sofa stands under the light. The sofa stands parallel to George's left side. The cushion lies in the corner of the sofa further away from George. The light is on. It's fairly weak. George follows Eleanor with his eyes. She goes up to the sofa. She lies down on it. She rests her head on the cushion. She puts her feet on the sofa. She crosses them. She puts her right foot over her left one. Her feet are nearly a foot away from the edge of the sofa. Eleanor puts her hands in her lap. They don't touch. Eleanor closes her eyes. Her clothes look very neat. This is especially true of her skirt. It's as if someone had arranged it after Eleanor's lying down. Because of the relative position of the sofa in respect to the light her face is clearly illuminated. This is so in spite of the light being fairly weak. Eleanor's face and mouth look the same as immediately after her reading George's writing. Because of the relative position of the sofa in respect to the light her cheekbones cast long shadows on her cheeks. Because of this the cheekbones look much higher than in reality. Because of this in turn the cheeks look hollower than in reality. Eleanor looks like Nefertiti.

DAPHNIS AND CHLOE

Oleh is George's friend. George has stayed with him for instance. Oleh is Ukrainian. He was born in the Ukraine. He was born in 1943. He lives in Canada now. He lives in Toronto. He came to Canada in 1949. He's a Canadian citizen. He's a photographer. He free-lances. His free-lance work consists primarily of fashion photography. He also does art photography. This consists primarily of portraits and nudes. The nudes include sex acts. Oleh exhibits and sells his art photography. He's a very good photographer. This applies to both his fashion- and art work. Oleh is also a partner in a discotheque right now. He supplements his income this way. He's doing very well financially. He was married. He was married from 1966 to 1969. He got divorced. He then lived with a girl. He lived with her from 1969 till 1973. Her name was Chloe. She was English. She was born in England. She was also a Canadian citizen. Oleh broke up with her in 1973. The story of the breakup is the following. In April of 1973 Oleh went to Europe. The purpose of the trip was vacation. Oleh went to visit a friend of his. The friend was also Ukrainian. He was also born in the Ukraine. He was also a Canadian citizen. He was an architect. He lived in Norway at the time. He was working on a project there. Oleh went alone. He flew into Amsterdam. He spent a few days there. He then took a train to Norway. This included a ferry ride from Denmark to Sweden. Oleh travelled around Norway with his friend. The friend was married. He had an infant son. The wife and son came along on the trip. They all went in Oleh's friend's car. Oleh enjoyed himself on the trip. He stayed in Norway two weeks. He'd come over on a fourteen-to-twenty-two day excursion trip. He was planning to fly back from Paris. He had another three days left. He flew over to Paris from Oslo. He spent the remainder of his time in Europe there. The day of the departure he met a girl. This was at the air terminal in Paris. The girl was French. She was a stewardess. Her name was Francoise. Oleh and Francoise liked each other. She flew frequently into Montreal. Oleh made frequent business trips to that city. He asked Francoise to give him a call during her next visit to Montreal. He said he'd meet her. He got home that day. This was May fourth. Chloe was gone. A friend of Oleh's was living at Oleh's place at the time. The friend was French Canadian. His name was Jean Jacques. Jean Jacques told Oleh what'd happened. Chloe was a fashion model. This is how she and Oleh had met. The night Oleh left Chloe brought a guy along to stay with her. The guy worked at the same fashion agency as Chloe. He was a designer. He stayed with Chloe in the apartment. He slept with her in Oleh's bed. Jean Jacques wanted to write to Oleh about this. Jean Jacques didn't do it however. He felt embarrassed. Oleh had a car. The guy and Chloe used the car. Two days before Oleh's coming back Chloe and the guy moved out. She left for Vancouver. Her family lived there. The guy stayed in Toronto. Oleh had a pair of elevated shoes. They were expensive. They were beautiful. They were Italian. The guy liked them. They fit him. Chloe gave them to him. He'd been wearing a pair of boots. They were badly worn. The guy left them behind. He left them in place of Oleh's shoes. Chloe took some of her things. She left most of them behind however. Oleh was very upset on discovering all this. The first thing he tried to do was to get in touch with Chloe. He called up her parents. Chloe was staying with a married sister of hers however. Oleh didn't want to call there. He didn't get along with the sister. He'd had an affair with her prior to meeting Chloe. This is how he'd met Chloe. He left a message for her to call him. She called him later that day. She called collect. This irked Oleh. Chloe said she was tired of living with him. She said he controlled her too much. She said she wanted to be her own person. She said she wanted to see what she could accomplish herself. She asked Oleh to hold the rest of her clothes for her. She said she'd pick them up later. Oleh and Chloe had two cats. The cats were Siamese. They were from the same litter. Their names were Tw and Ins. Chloe had left the cats with Oleh. She said over the phone she wanted them. She asked Oleh to send them to her. She'd loaned him five hundred dollars. She asked him to send it also to her. She said she needed the money. Oleh didn't commit himself to carrying out any of her wishes. He hinted he might not however. He hated and despised Chloe. He told her that. He tried to forget her after that. He plunged into work. He tried getting more jobs. This included industrial photography. Oleh was successful in this. He redecorated his apartment. He got a headboard for the bed. He got new curtains for the bedroom and living room. He had the sofa reupholstered. He painted the living room, hall, and kitchen. He covered parts of the walls with cloth. It was the same as in the upholstering on the sofa. Oleh got new chairs for the living-room table. The chairs came from a bankrupt discotheque. At this time Oleh also began having intercourse with a number of girls. One of these was Francoise. She happened to come to Montreal about two weeks after Oleh's return. She called Oleh up. He drove over to Montreal. He had intercourse with her that night. He kept seeing her on and off after that. Another girl he had intercourse with was Jeanette. She was French Canadian. She was from Quebec. She lived in Toronto. She was eighteen years old. She worked in a restaurant. She worked as a waitress. She spoke poor English. She was fairly pretty. She had a boy friend prior to meeting Oleh. She dropped the boy friend for Oleh. The boy friend tried to make trouble for Oleh. The boy friend was dissuaded from doing this by Jeanette and his other friends. One reason she dropped him for Oleh was because of Oleh's promising to make a fashion model out of her. He took pictures of her. He prepared a portfolio for her. He started showing the portfolio around. He met Jeanette at the time of George's staying at his place. He had intercourse with her the first time during George's staying at his place. George happened to be spending that night at another place however. One reason for this was his knowing Oleh planned to have intercourse with Jeanette that night. Still another girl Oleh had intercourse with was a Canadian Ukrainian. The girl was also eighteen years old. She was born in Canada. She spoke Ukrainian fluently however. As a matter of fact she spoke English with a Ukrainian accent. She was a fervent Ukrainian patriot. She was involved in the campaign to liberate Ukrainian dissidents. She tried to make a Ukrainian patriot out of Oleh. He liked her. He liked her the most of any Ukrainian girl he'd known. He'd started having intercourse with her a long time after George's visiting him. He had a number of telephone conversations with Chloe before, during, and after George's staying with him. He recorded these conversations on tape. He played some of them to George during George's stying with him. This was so because of George's and Oleh's having discussed Chloe. George was advising Oleh on how to behave toward her. In general George was recommending firmness. Oleh didn't send Chloe the five hundred dollars. This was the reason for most of the calls. Chloe had made most of the calls to Oleh. She wanted him to send her the money. She also wanted him to send her the cats. She said she missed them. Oleh however refused to send her the money. He said she hadn't been contributing to their household nearly as much as he. He said she owed him at least five hundred dollars. While painting the apartment he did some tidying up. In the course of this he came across a bond. It belonged to Chloe. It'd been hidden in the kitchen. The bond was for two hundred dollars. Oleh hadn't known about it. Chloe had bought it secretly. Oleh sent the bond to her. He told her this was in lieu of the five hundred dollars. He said he could have destroyed the bond if he'd wanted to. After a while Chloe apparently began living with a guy. She tried establishing herself as a model in Vancouver. She was making no headway however. She was broke. Eventually she came back to Toronto. This was ten months after her leaving Oleh. Chloe came to Toronto just for a visit. She was planning to go back to Vancouver. She was hoping to find somebody to give her a push in Toronto. She however was prepared to stay in Toronto in case a good opportunity for her came up. She had a few girl friends in Toronto. She called up one of the girl friends before coming to Toronto. Chloe was going to stay with that girl friend. Chloe arrived late at night. She went to her girl friend's place. It was closed. Chloe waited for about an hour. It was getting late. She didn't know what to do. She found a phone. She began calling up her other girl friends and friends. It was Friday night. None of the people were home. Chloe knew a bar her particular girl friend sometimes went to. Chloe went there. The girl friend wasn't there however. Chloe was desperate. She didn't have much money. She didn't want to go to a hotel. She thought of calling Oleh. She was afraid to do this. Eventually she called Oleh however. He was at home. He was in bed. He was in bed with Jeanette. Chloe asked him if she could come over and sleep on the sofa. He told her to come over. He told Jeanette to go home. He said a good friend of his was coming over. Oleh said he didn't want the friend to see Jeanette. She began crying. Oleh got angry. He threw her and her clothes out of the apartment. Chloe came to the apartment fairly soon thereafter. Oleh took her through the apartment. He showed her the improvements. He asked her what she thought of them. She said she liked them. She said she was very tired. She asked if she could go to sleep right away. She wanted to sleep on the sofa. Oleh got angry. He told Chloe to get into bed. She began crying. She said she didn't want to have intercourse with Oleh. She said she'd go away. Oleh got angrier. He pushed Chloe into the bedroom. He shouted at her to get into bed. He said he wasn't planning to have intercourse with her. He told her to take off her clothes. She obeyed him. She left her slip, brassiere, and underpants on however. Oleh shouted at her again. He told her to take off all her clothes. He sounded very threatening. Chloe obeyed him. He was partly dressed. He took off his clothes. He climbed into bed. He lay still for a while. He then turned toward Chloe. He pressed his body against hers. He lay this way for a long time. He didn't get an erection. After a while he spoke again. He told Chloe she was stupid. He said she could see he didn't care about her. He said she didn't even make him aroused. She was still shaking with fear. She began crying again. Oleh turned away from her. He went to sleep. He and Chloe didn't have intercourse that night. She called up her girl friend in the morning. Chloe went over to the girl friend's. Oleh and Chloe agreed however to see each other that afternoon. They did this. They went out. They drove in Oleh's car into the country. They had dinner together. Oleh paid for the dinner. He got a little high from drinking. He began crying. He said this was due to his father's being on the point of dying. This wasn't true however. Oleh's father was merely sick. Oleh told Chloe she should take her things out of his apartment. Oleh and Chloe went to his apartment. Most of her things were still in the closets. Oleh opened one of the closets. He told Chloe to pack her things. She asked him to wait. She said she'd get them some other time. Oleh got angry. He was wearing a belt. It was wide. It had a heavy buckle. Oleh took the belt off. He threatened Chloe with it. He said he'd beat her up if she didn't take her things out of the apartment. He swung the belt at her. He was aiming with the buckle. He hit Chloe on the shoulder with the buckle. The blow glanced off her however. This happened close to the kitchen door. Chloe jumped into the kitchen. There was a knife lying on the stove. Chloe grabbed the knife. She went after Oleh with it. He got scared. He was in the living room. The sofa was there. It stood in the middle of the room. Oleh was close to the sofa. He ran behind the sofa. Chloe stood on the other side of it. She stood opposite Oleh. She threatened him with the knife. He tried to calm her down. He also told her she should put the knife away. He said he could kill her. He said he could get away with this because of doing it in self defense. He finally persuaded Chloe to put the knife away. Only then did he get out from behind the sofa. The table in the living room was behind Chloe. She put the knife on the table. Oleh walked very slowly. He neared the table. He was holding the belt. He'd wrapped it around his fist. He was prepared to use the fist as a shield in case of being attacked by Chloe with the knife. He was watching her very carefully. He was afraid she'd grab the knife. On coming to the table he grabbed the knife. He did this very fast. He threw the knife under the sofa. He did this also very fast. He threw the belt away. He grabbed Chloe. He slapped her a few times on the face. His blows again glanced off her face however. Chloe began to scream. Oleh told her to shut up. He told her he'd kill her if she didn't. He pulled her into the bedroom. He threw her onto the bed. He threw himself on top of her. She was wearing a dress. Oleh lifted her dress. He began tearing her underpants off. He tore them. He managed to expose Chloe's crotch. He put his hand between her legs. He stuck his fingers inside her vagina. At first he stuck two fingers inside it. Eventually he stuck four of them in. He was nearly tearing Chloe's vagina apart. He was pleased to do this. He talked to Chloe all this time. He was telling her how she'd hurt him. She was no longer screaming. She was silent. She was terrified. She'd merely say "Yes" when Oleh expected her to do this. This was during her being accused of being guilty toward him. Chloe also complained of her vagina hurting. This was only in the beginning however. With time Chloe's vagina stretched apparently. Chloe also cried on and off. This was due to the fear and to her vagina hurting. With time Oleh noticed he had an erection. He noticed he was sexually very excited. He unzipped his pants. He took his penis out. He turned around so as to offer the penis to Chloe for sucking. He did this without taking his fingers out of her vagina. He told Chloe to take his penis in her mouth. He told her he'd tear her womb out and her vagina apart if she didn't. He attempted to put his fifth finger inside her vagina while saying this. Chloe began to scream at this point. This was again due to fear and pain. Oleh told Chloe to shut up. He spoke in a soothing voice. He was afraid Chloe wouldn't stop screaming. He was afraid he'd gone too far. He again told Chloe to take his penis in her mouth. She quieted down. She obeyed Oleh. It occurred to him she could bite his penis. He told her not to try doing this. He said he'd tear her vagina apart. He didn't try pushing his fifth finger inside her vagina however. Chloe however made no attempt at biting Oleh's penis. The thought had never entered her mind. Chloe was moving her mouth back and forth over Oleh's penis. This aroused Oleh more. This was because of his not having told Chloe to do this. Oleh hadn't planned to reach an orgasm this way. Now however he decided to do this. He urged Chloe to move her mouth more effectively. He told her to use her tongue for instance. She obeyed him in everything. He reached an orgasm. This took about fifteen minutes. Chloe swallowed Oleh's semen. She made no attempt at not doing this. Oleh's penis continued erect after the orgasm. Chloe had tried to take the penis out of her mouth after his orgasm. Oleh told her to keep it in however. He continued talking to her about how he was hurt. He kept moving his penis in and out of her mouth. This was so in order not to let the penis grow soft. This time Chloe hardly moved her mouth at all. Oleh noticed this. He however didn't criticize Chloe. He felt she'd done a good job already. He continued this for a while. Eventually his penis began to grow soft. Oleh noticed this. By then he also didn't feel he'd anything to say. He felt he'd gotten everything off his chest. He took his penis out of Chloe's mouth. He'd held it there for a total of about an hour. He took his fingers out of Chloe's vagina. He'd held them there for a total of about an hour and a half. He got off the bed. He zipped his pants up. Chloe was still on the bed. Oleh told her to get up. He said he'd drive her to her girl friend's. He said he'd get all her things together that night. He told Chloe to pick them up the next day. He said he'd throw them out otherwise. He said he'd keep the cats. He said everything was over between them. Chloe began crying again. Oleh kept uring her to get going. She'd been wearing a coat. Oleh got the coat. He threw it to Chloe. He told her to put it on. She did this. Oleh grabbed her arm. He led Chloe out of the apartment. She didn't put up any resistance. Oleh took her to his car. He wasn't speaking. He felt good. He felt elated. He got in the car. He opened the door for Chloe. She got inside. She was still crying. Oleh still felt good. He drove off. He drove for about ten minutes. He was nearing Chloe's girl friend's apartement. He was approaching an intersection. There was a traffic light there. The light turned red. Oleh stopped the car at the intersection. There was a street light at the intersection. The light was mercury vapor. The light was strong. It was illuminating the inside of the car very brightly. Oleh looked to his right. He saw Chloe. She was no longer crying. She stared ahead. Her face looked blank. Oleh remembered what Chloe had done to him. In an instant he was filled with anger again. He swung his right hand at Chloe. He hit her on the face. He did this pretty hard. Chloe screamed on being hit. She covered her face with her hands. She moved over to the side of the car. She however made no attempt at getting out. Oleh continued looking at her. He could see the part of her face not covered by the hands. The face looked very pale in the light. The face looked a little greenish. There was still a lot of snow in the streets. Oleh remembered the color of the snow. The face looked about the color of the snow to him. He saw something dark on Chloe's face between her fingers. The substance looked black. It seemed to move. It seemed liquid. Oleh assumed it was blood. He assumed he'd broken Chloe's nose or lip. He realized he'd overdone it. He was sorry to have done this. He felt some complications might develop from the incident. The idea seemed tedious. Oleh wished he'd dropped Chloe off without the incident. He wished he were back in his apartment.

INCIDENT IN THE DRIVEWAY

The driveway is fairly long. It's fairly narrow. It slopes up from the street. The driveway is paved with asphalt. There's a retaining wall on the left side of the driveway looking in from the street. The wall is made of stone. The wall is quite tall. It's more than six feet tall in some places. It's overgrown with ivy in most places. There's a car in the driveway. The car is a Volkswagen sedan. It's a 1967 model. The car is in good shape. The car is white. Its inside is black. The registration number of the car is 984.YRF. The registration is New York State. The license plate was put on the car less than an hour ago. The car is facing away from the street. The car is standing along the steepest part of the driveway. The car's engine is turned off. The left door of the car is open. The door blocks the space between the car and the retaining wall. There's a woman standing next to the door. She's standing on the street side of the door. She's thirty-seven years old. She's about five feet six inches tall. She weighs about one hundred and thirty pounds. Her hair is loose. It's long. It reaches to a little above the woman's waist. The hair is smoothly combed. The woman had combed the hair less than half an hour ago. The hair is brown. It's gray in places. The woman's face is oval. It's a little unsymmetrical. The woman's complexion is light. The woman has wrinkles on her forehead. Her nose is straight. It's fairly short. The woman's eyes are blue-gray. Her mouth is also unsymmetrical. Its corners are turned down a little. The woman wears no lipstick. She wears a sweater, body shirt, jeans, and sandals. The sweater is a cardigan. It's wool. It's heavy. It's handmade. It was made in Ireland. The body shirt has a low neck. The shirt has three-quarter-length sleeves. It's knitted. The material is thin. It's synthetic. It has a pattern. The pattern is floral. The flowers are large. They look like peonies. The colors of the shirt are orange, yellow, and white. The jeans are fairly new. They're a little faded however. This was accomplished artificially. The sandals have two strips running across the toes. The strips form an X. The sandals are rubber. They're white. The woman carries a handbag. It's a pouch in reality. The pouch is quite small. It's rectangular. It's about four inches by six inches. It's gathered by a string at one end. The pouch is made from a fabric. The fabric is cotton. The pouch was made in Mexico. The pouch has a pattern. The pattern is geometric. The pouch is pink and white. It's full. It bulges. The woman is holding it by the string. She's turned at an angle of about forty-five degrees toward the street. George is standing next to the woman. He is wearing a pullover, shirt, shorts, and shoes. The pullover has a zipper. The pullover has long sleeves. It's velour. It's dark red. The shirt is of the polo type. The shirt has three buttons. It has short sleeves. It's nylon. It's about the same color as the pullover. The shorts are of the hiking type. They have six pockets. There are four pockets up front. The other pockets are in the back. The pockets are very deep. They go down to the very edge of the legs of the shorts. The shorts are light beige. They're nearly white. They're faded from frequent washing. George had bought them from a mail-order house. The house is the L.I. Bean Company. The shoes are running shoes. They're the Nike Nylon Super Cortez model. Their uppers are nylon. The soles of the shoes are rubber. There are decorations on each side of each shoe. The decorations are in the shape of curved stripes. The stripes curve up at the ends. The stripes end in points. The stripes are plastic. The uppers are blue. The soles are white. So are the decorations. So finally are the laces. George had put the pullover on a few minutes ago. He'd done this because of feeling cold. This is so in spite of it being about seventy degrees and sunny. George is standing about four feet away from the woman. He's standing between her and the street. He's facing her. They've been arguing. The woman accuses George wrongly of something. He gets very angry. The emotions seem to grow inside him like gas expanding in a container. His body seems the container. George literally feels as if he's about to explode. He feels going away from the woman would ease the pressure inside him. He turns away. He walks to the edge of the road. A thought then enters his mind that he should strike the woman. He almost literally shakes at the thought. In this he's like a hungry man seeing food within his reach. George feels he shouldn't strike the woman. This is so because of his being afraid to get into legal trouble due to this. George can't resist the temptation to strike the woman however. There's no one around besides him and the woman. He knows this. He knows there'll be no witness to his striking the woman. This is one reason for his not being able to resist the temptation. He decides to strike the woman. He hopes she hasn't gotten inside the car. He turns around. The woman is closer to the car now. She's about to get inside it. George sees this. He's afraid of missing his chance. He speaks to the woman. He tells her to wait. He says he wants to tell her something. He speaks calmly. He hopes to change the woman's mind by this. The woman stops getting into the car on hearing him. She moves away from it. She gets back almost as far away from it as before. She turns at about the same angle to the car as before. George comes up to her. He comes up to within about two feet of her. He pretends to be clam. He plans to strike the woman with his right hand. He plans to strike her on the left cheek. His right hand is hanging down. George moves the hand partly behind his back. He does this in order for the hand to move faster on contact with the woman's cheek. He keeps his hand relaxed. He swings it toward the woman's left cheek. He applies a fair amount of force to the hand. He's not aware of the amount of the force. He wasn't planning to apply so much force. He strikes the woman on the left cheek. His hand is still relaxed. It strikes the cheek evenly. The cheek feels soft to George. This strikes him as pathetic. He feels a little sorry for the woman because of the softness of her cheek. He feels ashamed at feeling sorry. The hand makes a fairly loud noise on striking the cheek. George feels a stinging sensation in his hand. The sensation is hot and cold at the same time. The sensation is almost like that produced by scalding. It really is as if hot water had been poured over the palm of George's hand. The woman's cheek seems the water. George says: "You bitch!" on striking the woman. She's thrown off balance by the blow. She moves back. She falls onto the retaining wall. She seizes the top of the car door in the process. She does this with her left hand. She starts sliding down the wall. She slides down about a foot. She stops herself from falling by holding onto the wall with her right hand. She says: "Oh, my God!" She says this in a fairly low voice. She stands up immediately on stopping herself from falling. She holds her left cheek with her left hand. She moves very fast. She gets into the car. She starts looking in her pouch. She's looking for her keys. She finds them very soon. She tries to put the keys in the ignition lock. She's having difficulty doing this. George sees this. He knows the woman will try driving. He's afraid she'll try running him down. This is especially so because of the door being open. George fears the woman will try knocking him over by backing up with the door open. He also fears she might want to shoot him. He fears she has a gun in the car. He decides to flee. He decides to run home. He turns around. He starts running. He feels ashamed at doing this. He knows however he should flee. He hears the car engine start. He speed up. He runs fairly fast. He runs in long strides. He moves like an experienced runner. He's aware of this. This makes him feel better. This partly overshadows the shame he feels on fleeing. He reaches the street. He decides to get out of the path of the car as soon as possible. He crosses the street. He gets up onto the edge of the curb on the other side of the street. He turns right. He continues running. There's another street branching off to the left a few yards ahead. George steps down into this street. He crosses it. He gets up onto the curb. He feels fairly safe there. He feels the car wouldn't be very likely to run him down there. He's still ashamed of fleeing. He feels he should stop. He feels he should merely walk from then on. He feels the chances of his being run down by the car at that moment are small. He feels getting rid of the feeling of shame would be worth taking the risk of being run down by the car at this moment. He gives in to his desire. He starts walking. He turns his head right. He sees the car. The car is on the right side of the street. The car is moving forward. George is pacified by this. He knows he'd made the right decision as far as stopping to run is concerned. He slows down more. He relaxes more. He pretends to be completely calm. He continues looking at the car. He sees the woman. She's looking straight ahead. She seems not to be aware of George. She seems to have forgotten his existence. George is a little disappointed by this. He'd have liked the woman to show a sign of being aware of him. He'd have liked her to show fear of him or anger at him for instance. The car is moving fairly fast. George sees the woman primarily as a blur. It seems to consist of three colors. These are brown, white, and red. These colors correspond to those of the woman's hair, face, and sweater respectively. These colors seem streaks of paint. The streaks seem to have been made on the air above the street as if on a wall. George feels some affinity for the woman. He feels as if something related to him were moving away from him. He's not aware of the reason for this. The reason is the color of her sweater. The color of the sweater reminds George of the color of his pullover. He can see the pullover with his peripheral vision. It's as if his pullover were being driven away from him. It's therefore as if George were being driven away from himself. The car moves past him. It continues driving in the same direction and at the same speed. George feels completely safe. He's glad at having struck the woman. He becomes aware of a stinging sensation in his right hand. This is especially true of the tips of his fingers. It's as if the tips were being pinched. It's as if there were an object attached to them. The object could be a clothes pin clamped to the finger tips for instance. The object could also be something small glued to the fingertips. It could be a wooden match for instance. In this case the pinching would be due to the glue puckering up the skin on drying. George realizes he'd struck the woman harder than he'd planned. He's glad to have done this however. He knows he hasn't marked the woman in any way. He knows he hadn't hit her on the nose causing it to bleed for instance. He sees everything has turned out for the best. He feels that when the chips are down this is always the case with him.

SISTER OF SNAKES

It was early fall. It was in the woods. The foliage had just started to turn yellow. Jim Morrison was a long-distance runner. He ran every day. He was taking his daily run. He was running along a dirt road. It sloped gently up. Jim Morrison had just come around a curve. He then saw a snake. It was about six feet away from him. It was in the middle of the road. The snake was fairly small. It was about two feet long. It was about three quarters of an inch in diameter. The snake was black. It had a design on its back. Jim Morrison managed to see a little of the design. It was geometric. It was white. It gave the snake the appearance of a telephone cable. This was especially so because of the snake's being black. The design also gave the snake the appearance of a ladies' laced boot. The design was like a white shoe lace going down the front of the boot. The snake had raised about the front half of its body off the ground. The mouth of the snake was open. The mouth was tiny. It was dark red. It looked like an overripe raspberry. The raspberry seemed partly crushed. The snake seemed to hold the rapsberry in its mouth. The snake was hissing. Its tongue was vibrating. It seemed the tongue made the hissing noise. The tongue looked like a little flame. The flame seemed made of flesh. The snake's top two fangs were also visible. They were thin. They were white. They looked like two nerves. The snake was swaying from side to side. Jim Morrison stopped on seeing the snake. He felt terrified. He was bare-legged. He was afraid of running past the snake. He was sure it'd bite one of his calves during his passing it. He could almost feel the fangs sinking into his flesh. The sensation was frightening. After a few seconds the snake began to move toward Jim Morrison. It did this without lowering the front half of its body. The snake was somehow managing to move along on the back half of its body. It was clear to Jim Morrison the snake was going after him. He began to back away. There were bushes and trees along the road. Soon Jim Morrison found himself among them. At one point something began blocking his way. Jim Morrison assumed it was a branch of a bush or tree. He put his hand back. He wanted to bend the branch out of the way. He found two branches behind him. He put his other hand back. He grabbed the branches. They were quite thick. Jim Morrison could hardly put his fingers around them. The branches were also quite smooth. Jim Morrison tried to bend them out of the way. They didn't yield much however. Jim Morrison felt they were actually trunks of little trees. He felt it'd be easier to pull the trees out of the ground. He tried doing this. At first he was having some success. Then things got more difficult. Jim Morrison struggled with the trees. They wouldn't come out of the ground. Jim Morrison wanted to know the reason for this. He looked at the ground behind him. He saw the trees coming out of the ground. He saw the ground clinging to their roots like something viscous. The ground was like the membrane around the viscera of a living being. Jim Morrison seemed to be pulling part of the being's viscera out of the being. The sight was sickening. At that point Jim Morrison noticed the roots weren't roots at all. He noticed they were actually snakes. The snakes were very thick. They were grayish-black. They were shiny. Their skin looked like the bark of certain trees. Jim Morrison realized at this point he wasn't holding onto tree trunks. He realized he was holding onto bodies of huge snakes. The snakes were soft. Jim Morrison's fingers had sunken into their bodies. Jim Morrison felt the snakes writhing in his hands. He knew the snakes were doing this in order to free themselves. He knew they wanted to attack him. He became extremely terrified. He looked up behind him. He saw the thicket of trees there. He noticed then they weren't trees at all. He realized they were all snakes. The sight was positively terrifying. The space was all dark. Some of the snakes were as tall and thick as tree trunks. The snakes were all writhing. They all seemed to want to attack Jim Morrison. At this point he was sure the little snake had gotten to him. He was sure it was about to attack him. He turned his head around. He lowered his eyes. He saw the little snake. It was about a foot away from him. The snake was still raised. It was clearly about to strike at one of Jim Morrison's legs. Jim Morrison became terrified even more. He prepared himself to scream. A thought passed then through his mind that this couldn't be reality. Jim Morrison was sure it was only a dream. This was so because of his feeling he would have been attacked long ago by the snakes behind him if they were real. Also, he felt there could never be so many snakes in real life. Also, finally, he felt snakes couldn't be as big in real life as some of the ones he'd seen behind him. He relaxed then instantly. He could still see the little snake before him. He could also still feel the two snakes writhing in his hands. None of this however any longer terrified him. The sensations then became less vivid. They seemed to be blown away by a wind like fog or smoke. In this Jim Morrison now saw a proof of his supposition being correct. He then began to feel himself become awake. This also was happening gradually. Jim Morrison's becoming awake seemed like a different kind of fog or smoke being carried toward him by a wind. Eventually the dream dissipated completely. Jim Morrison felt himself completely awake. He became aware of the reason for his dream. A few days ago he'd come across a snake on his daily run. The surroundings had been like those in the dream. The snake had looked also like the one in the dream. The snake had been somewhat smaller however. It'd been about a foot and a half long. The snake hadn't been standing up in the middle of the road however. The snake had been lying down in the grass at the side of the road. Jim Morrison had run past the snake. He'd noticed it. He'd thought it was a piece of telephone cable. He'd been intrigued by this. He'd stopped. He'd turned around. He'd walked back to the snake. He'd seen it was a snake. It had seemed asleep. This was probably due to it being so late in the year. Jim Morrison had wanted to find out if the snake was alive. He'd gotten a twig. It'd been very thin. Jim Morrison had touched the snake with it. The snake had then moved. It'd raised its head. The snake had opened its mouth. The snake's mouth had looked like that of the snake in the dream. The snake had seemed to want to attack Jim Morrison. He'd been a little frightened. He'd felt like molesting the snake however. He'd touched it with the twig a few more times. The snake had then turned around. It'd crept off into the grass. The snake had done this very fast. Jim Morrison lay in his bed. He lay on his back. It was fairly cool in the room. Jim Morrison was covered up to his chin by the blanket. His arms were stretched out along his body. His feet were together. The room had two windows. The shades on the windows were up. It was at night. Some light was coming in from the street through the windows. It was fairly easy to see inside the room. Jim Morrison could see the two posts at the foot of the bed. They rose about six inches above the mattress. Jim Morrison could also see the chair in the left corner of the room. He could also see the dresser in the right corner of the room. He could see the two candle sticks, the jewelry box, and the toilet-water bottle on top of the dresser. He could also see the picture above the dresser. He could also finally see the chair against the wall on the right of the bed. He could see all these things without moving his head and practically even his eyes. The furniture was wooden. It was stained brown. It wasn't varnished. It was well-waxed however. It shone therefore a little in the light coming in from the street. The furniture did this like human eyes. The door to the room was on the right of the chair on the right of the bed. The door was open. Jim Morrison couldn't see it. He however was also aware of it. He was aware of its being open. His bedroom was on the second floor. There were three other rooms on this floor in addition to his bedroom. Two of these rooms were empty. The furniture had been taken out of these rooms recently. Jim Morrison had gotten divorced recently. The furniture had been taken by his former wife. Jim Morrison was also aware of this.

THE FIRST HAIR TRANSPLANT

The transplant takes place at a doctor's office. The doctor is one of the pioneers of hair transplants. The transplant is performed by another doctor however. This doctor is an assistant to the first doctor. The first doctor no longer performs many hair transplants. He devotes most of his time to research on a cure for baldness. The first doctor has another assistant. The three doctors are incorporated as a medical group. The name of the group contains that of the first doctor. George has had to wait for over three months for his appointment. The primary reason for this is the office having been closed during the summer for vacation. One has to wait nearly that long during the rest of the year for an appointment however. This is Thursday, September twentieth. The appointment is for 9:15 A.M. George comes in at 9:10 A.M. There's no one in the waiting room. There's a young man standing at the reception desk. There are three nurses behind the desk. There's no one talking to the man. One of the nurses is busy. The man is apparently being taken care of by this nurse. George goes up to the reception desk. One of the nurses comes up to him. She asks him if she can help him. He gives her his name. He says he has a 9:15 appointment with the assistant doctor. The nurse checks in the appointment book. For a while she seems not to be able to verify George's statement. George becomes worried. He asks if the nurse really can't find the appointment. She then finds the appointment. She says it's all right. She tells George to wait in the waiting room. He's relieved. He goes into the waiting room. He sits down in one of the chairs. He carries an attache case and a legal document folder. The attache case contains some papers and a magazine. The folder contains a manuscript. George has just finished working on the manuscript. It's a novel. The manuscript is very large. It's 575 typewritten pages long. It barely fits in the folder. George puts the attache case on his lap. He puts the folder on top of the attache case. He opens the folder. The manuscript is in a box. The box is paper. There's a rubber band pulled around its outside. George takes out the box. He takes off the rubber band. He opens the box. He begins looking through the manuscript. He goes to page four. This is where the text begins. George starts reading. He reads nearly to the bottom of the page. He likes the writing. By then about two minutes have passed since his starting to read. George then hears his name being called from the reception desk. He jerks. He calls out. He says he's coming. He puts the three front pages on top of the manuscript. He closes the box. He pulls the rubber band around it. He puts the box in the folder. He closes the folder. He gets up. He goes to the reception desk. The nurse who'd waited on him tells him to go to room number one. She points out its location. The room is deep inside the premises. George goes to it. It's tiny. It's about ten feet by six feet. It's painted off-white. The white is a little beige. The room has a door. The door is in one of the narrower walls. The door is of the swinging type. This is due to the smallness of the room. The door doesn't quite reach to the floor or the lintel. The door has two wings. They're of equal width. The door is made like a jalousie. The door is wooden. The wood is natural color and finish. The wood is pale. There's a light on the ceiling in the room. The light is fluorescent. There's a sink in the near left corner of the room in respect to the door. There's a mirror above the sink. There are ledges and cabinets along the two longer walls. The ledges and cabinets don't quite reach the wall with the door in it. There's a chair standing in the middle of the room. The chair faces the door. The frame of the chair is metal. The frame is chrome-plated. The chair has arm rests and a back. The arm rests are also metal. The back and seat of the chair are upholstered. They're upholstered in plastic. It's about the same color as the walls. There are two nurses in the room. They both look in their mid twenties. One of the nurses is white. She's about five feet seven. Her hair is long. It's straight. It reaches to about her shoulders. It's blond. The other nurse is black. She looks like a Filipino. She's about five feet four. She's petite. Her hair is straight. It's combed back smoothly. It's tied in a bun at the back of the head. George comes into the room. The black nurse is standing at the ledge on the right. She's looking at some papers. The white nurse is standing behind the chair. She's facing George. She tells him to bare the upper part of his body. He puts the attache case and the folder in the left near corner of the room in respect to the door. He puts them on the floor. He stands them on their edges. He puts the case and folder parallel to the wall on the left. He puts the folder between the wall and the attache case. He does this for the folder not to fall. He leans the folder against the wall. He wears a suit, tie, and shirt. He takes off his jacket. There's a hanger on the wall to the left of the door. George hangs up the jacket on the hanger. He takes off his tie. He drapes the tie over the left shoulder of the jacket. He takes off his shirt. He hangs it over the jacket. The white nurse tells him to sit down in the chair. He does this. The white nurse wraps a piece of bandage around his neck. The bandage is thick. It seems to have cotton in it. The nurse fastens the bandage in the back with an adhesive. She next wraps a plastic sheet over the upper part of George's body. The sheet fits like a poncho. It covers George's arms and lap. The plastic is thin. It isn't smooth. The depressions in it look like the pores in human skin. This is for the plastic to prevent liquid from flowing freely down it. The plastic is the color of very light coffee with cream. The plastic is nearly the color of a white person's skin. George sits straight while the nurse wraps the two things around him. His hands lie on the arm rests. George is holding firmly onto the arm rests. The veins on his hands and forearms bulge out. George continues sitting this way after the nurse is through with him. He sits in this fashion for a few more minutes. The nurses in the meantime are working. They spend most of their time behind George's back. George therefore doesn't see them most of the time. When he does see them they're merely walking. He therefore doesn't know what they're doing. He assumes they're making preparations for the transplant. He's right. The doctor who'll perform the transplant then appears. George has seen him during his consultation visit. George recognizes him. The doctor is fairly young. He looks younger than George. The doctor looks about thirty. He's fairly short. He's shorter than George. The doctor is fairly thin. He's about as thin as George. The doctor's hair is long. It's thick. It seems possible the hair has been transplanted. It's blond. The doctor wears a smock and pants. The smock is fairly short. It has long sleeves. It's white. The pants are fairly narrow. They have cuffs. The pants are black. The doctor greets everyone. George greets the doctor back. The doctor goes behind George. The doctor looks at George's head. He speaks with the nurses. He gives them instructions. He then walks out. George sits as before the doctor's appearance. The nurses also behave as before the doctor's appearance. This lasts for another few minutes. The doctor then reappears. He doesn't say anything this time. He again goes behind George. George feels the doctor snip hair from the back of his head. It's the lower right occipital region. The white nurse says to George it's going to hurt a little. She begins spraying his head with ethyl chloride. This is on the right front part of the top of the head. The spray feels cold. The sensation is slightly painful. The doctor then begins to jab the sprayed-on area with a needle. He's injecting local anesthetic. George feels a slight pain at first. After a few seconds he stops feeling it. He continues feeling the needle however. It seems to be jabbing into something frozen. It seems as if George's scalp were frozen solid. George seems to hear the kind of noise as from jabbing a needle into a block of ice. The noise also seems like the scratching of a needle on glass. The noise also seems like the crunching of ice or broken glass under one's feet. The doctor jabs the top of George's head for about fifteen seconds. He then warns George it's going to be more painful next. The nurse begins spraying the area from which the hair was cut in the back of the head. The doctor then begins to jab the area with the needle. George gives a slight moan on this happening. The area really is much more sensitive than the top of the head. The pain also gets weaker after a while. The pain however never stops as at the top of the head. Otherwise the jabbing of the needle feels identical to that at the top of the head. The doctor jabs the needle in this area about as long as at the top of the head. For a few seconds nothing is done to George. The doctor then begins to cut out the plugs to be transplanted. They're in the area in the back of the head. George feels the pressure of the instrument on his skull. The instrument is like a punch. George hears the noise of the skin being cut. He thinks the doctor is pulling out each plug after cutting it out. The doctor is merely cutting out the plugs however. The instrument makes a crunching noise similar to the needle before. At first George isn't disturbed by the noise. After a while however he begins to feel faint. He imagines the instrument cutting out his skin. He imagines the pieces of skin being torn up. Sweat stands out on his body. George hears ringing in his ears. He feels queasy. He says he's afraid he's going to faint. The white nurse tells him to keep his eyes open. After a few seconds the black nurse gives him a piece of bandage. It's folded into a wad. The bandage is soaked with ammonia. The black nurse tells George to bring the bandage close to his nose. She tells him to breathe deeply. She's on his left side. George takes the bandage in his left hand. He brings the bandage close to his nose. He begins to breathe in the ammonia. It's strong. It smells unpleasant. George's attention is attracted by the smell of ammonia. George no longer feels he's going to faint. This is so in spite of his not feeling better. It's as if fainting were falling asleep. It's as if the smell of the ammonia were preventing George from falling asleep like a noise. In the meantime the doctor moves the instrument to the top of George's head. He proceeds working there. The top of the head feels to George identical to the back. The white nurse asks him how he feels. He says he still feels queasy. The nurse asks him if he's had any breakfast. He says he has. He adds he's eaten very little however. The nurse then says she'll give him a Coke. She says the sugar in the Coke will help him feel better. In the meantime the doctor has finished working. He speaks to the nurses. George doesn't hear what the doctor says. The doctor leaves the room. The black nurse hands George a Coke bottle. It has a straw in it. George takes the bottle in his right hand. He takes a sip out of the bottle. He doesn't usually drink soft drinks. This is especially true of Colas. This is so because of them having caffein and sucrose. The last time George had a Cola is close to ten years ago. He likes the taste of the Coke however. He doesn't feel guilty drinking the Coke. This is so because of his needing it. George therefore feels this is one of the benefits of the transplant. At this point the white nurse starts working on top of his head. She removes the plugs of skin cut out by the doctor. She does this with a pair of tweezers. She pries the plugs up at first. She then tears them off. She does this rapidly. George feels the nurse working. He feels the tugging at his scalp. He doesn't know what it is. He's too tired to think about it. The areas from which the plugs were removed bleed. After a while George feels faint again. This is due to the bleeding. George isn't aware of the bleeding however. He places the bandage with ammonia to his nose. He also drinks some Coke. The white nurse notices this. She asks George how he feels. He replies he feels bad. The nurse says he's breathing too fast. She tells him to breathe slower. She tells him to fill his lungs completely with each breath. She also tells him to take more ammonia into his lungs. He tries this. He feels better. The white nurse finishes working on the top of his head. She goes away from George. The black nurse places a wad of bandage on top of his head. She says she'll need one of his hands for a while. George transfers the bandage with ammonia to his right hand. He continues holding the Coke bottle with the same hand. He lifts his left hand. The black nurse takes it. She places it over the bandage. She tells George to press down. He does this. He overdoes this a little. His head feels wooden. The feeling is unpleasant. The white nurse in the meantime begins working on the back of George's head. She does the same thing there as on the top of his head. She asks George to bend his head down a little. He does this. He again feels the tugging at his scalp. After a while he again feels faint. This is due to the same reason as the previous time. George notices he's breathing quite fast. He begins breathing slower. He brings the bandage with ammonia close to his nose. He then drinks some Coke. He repeats the process a few times. The white nurse apparently notices his behavior. She apparently notices his slow breathing. She tells George to keep his eyes open. He notices his eyes are nearly closed. He opens them wide. He realizes the nurse couldn't know his eyes were nearly closed. He realizes she said this just in case they were. He thinks her intelligent. She finishes working on the back of his head. She puts a wad of bandage on the back of his head. She tells George to take his hand off the bandage on the top of his head. The bandage stays in place. The white nurse wraps an ace bandage around the sides of George's head. This keeps the bandage in the back of his head in place. This also partly keeps the bandage on the top of his head in place. The ace bandage is tight. George finds the feeling pleasant. The white nurse then leaves him alone. He puts the bandage with ammonia in his left hand. He sits this way. He does this for a few minutes. He's beginning to feel better. At one point he happens to look to his right. The black nurse is sitting there by the ledge. There's a dish next to her. It has little round pieces of flesh with hair on them. They're bloody. They seem bloody to George the way a severed head would. The black nurse picks up one of them with tweezers. She begins working on it. George can't tell what she's doing. He realizes the pieces are a part of him. He feels very faint. He turns his head away from the ledge. He gives out a moan. He says he's going to faint. The white nurse tells him to breathe deeply. She tells him to smell the ammonia. She tells him to keep his eyes open. He does all this. The white nurse says she'll let him lie down. The back of the chair folds back. The nurse lowers the back partially. George lies back. The nurse puts the waste can in front of the chair. She tells George to put his feet up on the can. He does this. He tries to smell the ammonia and drink Coke at the same time. The straw doesn't quite reach the level of the Coke in the bottle. George merely sucks some air in when drawing on the straw. He tilts the bottle up more. Some of the liquid spills out onto his face. George doesn't like this. He wipes the Coke off his face with the right hand. He tilts the bottle up again. He sits up a little. He lowers the straw in the bottle. He gets some Coke then. He lies back.

After that he learns to drink out of the bottle while lying down. He does this by tilting his head sideways and bringing the bottle closer to his lips. He feels better after a while. At one point he's reminded of Kafka's "In the Penal Colony." The sweetness of the Coke reminds him of the taste of the gruel as described in the story. He asks the nurses if they've read the story. Only the black nurse answers. She says she hasn't. She asks what the story is about. George explains. Both nurses laugh. At about this point the white nurse tells George he'll have to sit up. She asks him how he feels. He answers he feels all right. The nurse puts the back of the chair up in a vertical position. She takes off the ace bandage and the bandage on top of George's head. She proceeds working on the top of his head. She's putting in the plugs. George can't feel this. He assumes however the nurse is putting in the plugs. She finishes her work after about two minutes. George finishes the Coke at about the same time. He puts the bottle on the chair next to him. He stands the bottle up. He puts it on his right side. He makes sure the bottle won't fall over. He presses it to the arm rest with his right thigh. The black nurse asks his pardon at about this time. She says she has to use the waste can. George lifts his legs up. He has to tense up his stomach muscles to do this. The black nurse raises the lid of the can. She throws something into the can. George sees it. It seems to him to consist of bandages and something pink. He assumes the pink stuff to be the plugs from the top of his head. He feels sick at the thought. The sickness is almost purely emotional however. George doesn't feel he has to have his feet up on the can any longer. He tells the nurse to take it away. She does this. She puts the can in its original place. George doesn't put his feet down right away after that. He likes the feeling of his stomach muscles being tight. He likes exercising in general. He knows he won't be able to exercise for a few days after the transplant. He therefore is trying to use this opportunity to get some exercise in. After a few seconds he remembers the reason for his not being able to exercise after the transplant. It is because of exercise raising the blood pressure. This might cause the plugs to be pushed out. George realizes this is the worst time to exercise. This is so because of the plugs having been just put in. George therefore lowers his legs. He isn't worried. He feels confident he hadn't raised his blood pressure enough to hurt the plugs. He puts his feet on the floor. He sits relaxed. He sits this way for a few minutes. The doctor comes in at this time. He doesn't say anything. He again goes behind George. The doctor looks at George's head. He taps the back of the head. This is to test if it'll bleed. The doctor speaks to the nurses. He says everything looks fine. He leaves the room. The white nurse then speaks to George. She says she'll put a few sutures in the back of his head. She says he should take them out in about four days. She says he could come into the office or have someone at home do this. She then proceeds putting the sutures in. George feels the thread pulling on his scalp. The scalp feels tight. The feeling is unpleasant. The nurse finishes putting in the sutures. She puts a dressing over the top and back of George's head. She attaches the dressing with an adhesive. She bandages George's head. The bandaging takes a long time. George feels the bandage accumulate on his head. The bandage does this like grayness. The bandage forms a turban. George isn't sure of this. He feels the top of his head might be exposed. He hopes this isn't true. The bandage feels warm. It also feels tight. The feeling is pleasant. George's ears are left exposed. The black nurse takes the plastic sheet off George. The white nurse cleans his nape with a wet piece of bandage. She washes off the blood that's accumulated there. George feels this. He realizes what's happening. The nurse finishes washing up. George gives the bandage with ammonia and the Coke bottle to her. She takes them. She goes away from George. He sits still. After a while the white nurse goes to the waste can. She throws the plastic sheet and a heap of bandages into the can. The bandages seem perfectly clean to George. He looks to the left. The black nurse is sitting by the ledge there. There are papers before her. She's writing something down. The white nurse comes back to George. His hair is long in the back. The hair sticks out from under the bandage. The white nurse combs George's hair. She tells George she's put two sutures in. He isn't sure when he should take them out. He asks the nurse this. She says it should be in about four days. She then says he should probably do it after washing his hair. She says it would be in five days. George has been told this during the consultation. He remembers this. The white nurse says he should take the sutures out then because his hair will be all caked up in that area prior to that. He plans to have the nurse at work take out the sutures. The white nurse reminds him the bandage should be taken off the next day. He's also been told this during the consultation. He also remembers this. The white nurse also reminds him to apply ointment to the surgical areas after the bandage is off. He's also been told this during the consultation. He also remembers this. At this point the black nurse walks out of the room. She takes some papers with her. The white nurse tells George he can get up. She tells him he can get dressed. She then also walks out of the room. She takes the Coke bottle with her. George gets up. He goes to the hanger. As was said, there's a sink and mirror in that corner of the room. George looks in the mirror. He sees his whole head is covered with the bandage. He's pleased by this. He thinks he looks attractive. His face is tanned. George thinks he looks like a Hindu. He smiles. He turns away from the mirror. He dresses. He looks in the mirror a few times while dressing. He picks up the attache case and folder on finishing dressing. He looks in the mirror again. He's still pleased with his appearance. He thinks if he weren't getting a hair transplant he'd wear a turban. He thinks this is a good way of hiding baldness. He walks out of the room. He goes to the reception desk. He lays the attache case and folder on top of the desk. He'd been asked to pay for the consultation visit on leaving the doctor's office at that time. He assumes he'll have to pay now too. He's carrying his check book in the attache case. He opens the attache case. He takes out the check book. There's a nurse behind the reception desk. She's white. The nurse is different from the one in the operating room however. There's another man in addition to George at the reception desk. The man is different from the one at the reception desk earlier in the morning. The nurse is waiting on the man. Another nurse comes up to the reception desk. She's black. This black nurse is different from the black nurse in the operating room. This nurse is definitely Negroid. She asks for George's name. George tells it to her. There are papers on the table behind the reception desk. The nurse looks at them. She picks up a few sheets held together by a paper clip. They look to George like the sheets the black nurse in the operating room had taken with her. He's not sure about this however. The nurse starts writing something on the sheets. George asks her how many plugs he'd received. She says it was fifteen. George had been told he should pay five dollars per plug plus twenty-five dollars each time. He remembers this. He calculates the figure. It comes out to be one hundred. George prepares himself to pay this amount. He starts filling out the stub of the check. He decides not to fill out the amount however in case of his being wrong. He remembers from his previous visit the checks should be made out to the medical group. He writes this name on the stub. He proceeds filling out the check. He makes it out to the medical group. He also doesn't fill out the amount on the check. He also doesn't sign the check. He waits for the nurse to finish. She finishes soon thereafter. There's a shelf on the side of the reception desk. There's medicine stored on the shelf. The medicine is stored in envelopes, bottles, jars, etc. The nurse goes up to the shelf. She gets a jar off the shelf. George suspects the jar contains the ointment. He's glad this is so. He was afraid he was going to get a prescription. He would have hated to have to go to a pharmacy to get the ointment. He also assumes he won't have to pay for the ointment separately. He's also glad at this. The nurse hands the container and one of the pieces of paper to him. The container is cylindrical. It's about an inch and a half tall. The container is also about as wide in diameter. The container is plastic. It's white. It has a label on top. The label has some words written on it. The words are "NEO-D OINTMENT APPLY TWICE DAILY TO SURGICAL AREAS." The words are written on two lines. The name of the medical group appears on the line below. The piece of paper is the width of a normal page. The piece of paper however is only about four inches long. It's grayish. It's the bill. George suspects this. The nurse tells him he owes one hundred and two dollars. He looks at the bill. He sees the figure written out there. He's surprised. He's disappointed. He asks the nurse how she's arrived at this figure. He says it should be one hundred. The nurse says he owes five dollars per plug, plus twenty-five dollars per visit, plus two dollars for the ointment. He sees in one instant her figure is correct. He's embarrassed at his behavior. He begs the nurse's pardon. He says he'd forgotten about the ointment. He blushes a little. He's also disappointed at having to pay for the ointment. He feels it could have been given to him free with the other charges being so high. He doesn't say anything however. He writes out the figure on the check. He signs the check. He fills out the figure on the stub. The balance above is 1519.29. George subtracts the figure on the stub from the balance above. He gets the balance of 1417.29. He tears off the check. He gives it to the nurse. He transfers the new balance to the next stub. He closes the check book. He puts it in the attache case. He also puts the ointment and bill in the attache case. He closes the attache case. He picks up the attache case and the folder. He says good-bye to the nurse. He turns away from the reception desk. He goes to the outside door. He goes outside. The day is beautiful. It reminds George of the day of the consultation visit. This was in the spring. George therefore feels as if it were spring. This is so even though the foliage on the trees has started to turn yellow. George is on Fifth Avenue. The office is located between Seventy-Third and Seventy-Second Street. George walks down to the Seventy-Second Street corner. He turns left. He walks along Seventy-Second Street. He knows there's a Rive-Gauche store on Madison Avenue nearby. He thinks the store is between Seventy-Second and Seventy-First Street. The store is between Seventy-First and Seventieth Street in reality. George plans to go to the store. He remembers having seen some nice clothes in the store a few years ago. They were very sporty-looking. Some of them were jump suits. George likes this kind of clothes. He'd like to buy some for himself. He worries however this type of clothes is no longer carried by the store. This is so because of his not having seen this type of clothes either on people or advertised anywhere for years. George decides to go to the store however. He knows the store is on the east side of Madison Avenue. On coming to the Madison Avenue corner he looks at the buildings on the east side of Madison Avenue between Seventy-Second and Seventy-First Street. He sees the store isn't there. He concludes the store must be between Seventy-First and Seventieth Street. He looks at the buildings on that side of the street in that block. He sees something that could be the store. The light is green for him to cross Madison Avenue. He crosses Madison Avenue. He has to wait for the light to change. The light turns green for him to cross Seventy-Second Street. He crosses Seventy-Second Street. He walks down to Seventy-First Street. The light is red his way. There are no cars coming however. George crosses the street. He goes up to the store. He sees himself reflected in the window. This is the first time he's seen himself reflected in a store window after leaving the doctor's office. The primary reason for this is that there'd been very few stores along the route he'd walked. He likes the way he looks. He likes the contrast of the bandage with his suit. He feels he looks even more like a Hindu. He looks at the clothes inside the store. They're hanging on racks. The clothes look mostly like women's clothes. George can't be sure about this however. This is so because of the current fashion. George is afraid the store carries only women's clothes now. He's afraid there's no Rive-Gauche men's store in town. He's afraid at the very best the men's store may be somewhere else. He decides to go into the store however. He does this. There are three girls inside the store. They're together. Two of them seem sales girls. One of them seems a customer. George walks around the racks. He looks at the clothes. They seem even more like women's clothes to him than before. He's worried even more than before. One of the girls seeming a sales girl looks at him. He catches her eye. He's embarrassed by this. He walks up to the girl. He asks her if the store carries men's clothes. She answers in the negative. She says the store carries only women's clothes. She says their men's store is between Fifty-Third and Fifty-Fourth Street. She doesn't say what avenue the store is on. George assumes it's Madison Avenue. He's right.

A CAR ACCIDENT

It's Tuesday. It's October the second. It's about six-forty in the evening. It's dark already. George is in his car. He's driving. The car is a 1970 Volkswagen squareback. It's white. George wears a jacket, sweater, pants, belt, and boots. The jacket is a sports jacket. It has one row of buttons. The jacket is cut in at the waist. The jacket has two vents in the back. The jacket has four pockets on the outside. Three of these are the usual pockets. The fourth one is a pocket for matches. This pocket is above the pocket on the right side. All the pockets on the outside have flaps. The jacket is made from camel's-hair cloth. The cloth is fairly thin. It's natural color. The buttons are leather. They're brown. The jacket was tailor-made in Spain. This was in the summer of 1967. The sweater is of the turtle-neck type. The sweater is made from a synthetic fibre. The sweater is fairly thin. It's dark red. The belt loops on the pants are fairly narrow. The pockets on the pants are up front. The fly in the pants has buttons instead of a zipper. The pants have thin legs. The pants have no cuffs. The pants are made from a whipcord cloth. It's wool. It's fairly thick. It's military green. The pants were made to match the jacket. They were made at the same place and time as the jacket. The belt is leather. It's dark brown. The buckle of the belt is plain. The buckle is golden. The belt was made in Spain. The belt was given to George as a Christmas present in 1964 in Spain. The boots are tall. They reach to just below the knees. The boots have rounded toes. The boots have slightly elevated heels. The boots have zippers on the inside of the calves. The boots have false laces up front. The boots are leather. They're dark red. The red is a little darker than that of the sweater. The boots were made in Italy. George bought them in New York. He bought them in 1972. He has a raincoat in the car. The raincoat lies on the back seat. The raincoat is of a military cut. The raincoat has a wide collar and lapels. The raincoat has shoulder patches. It has a vent in the back. The raincoat is fairly long. It's made from cotton suede. The material is cocoa-brown. The raincoat has one row of buttons. There are three of them. The raincoat has also one button on each shoulder patch. The buttons are round. They're flat. They have holes in the center. The buttons are metal. They're nearly black. The raincoat was made in France. George bought the raincoat at the same place and time as the boots. He's been driving along the West Side Highway. He's been driving downtown. He comes to the Nineteenth-Street exit. He takes that exit. He was planning to take that exit. The road is blocked off ahead anyway. This is due to the highway being repaired. George drives down the ramp. He finds himself under the elevated highway. There's a road under it. The road has two lanes. The traffic on it is permitted to go in the downtown direction only. The road is cobblestoned. There's a road running parallel to the road under the highway. The second road is on the left of the first one. The second road is no longer under the highway. There are quite a few cars on both roads. This is especially true of the first road. The cars on the first road are stopped directly beyond the ramp. George has to stop his car immediately after getting off the ramp. The cars ahead of him move ahead after about a minute and a half. He's planning to turn onto Fourteenth Street. He follows the cars. He's in the left lane. There are two traffic lights on the pillars on the left. The lights are green. George drives along. He comes to Fourteenth Street. There's a light on the pillar on the left at that street. The light is green. The car ahead of George slows down. He thinks it'll make a left turn. He's impatient for the car to do this. It continues straight however. It speeds up on reaching the intersection. George feels relieved to have the road free ahead. He also speeds up. He signals a left turn. He turns. He comes to the right lane of the second road. He hears a horn blowing at that instant. He also hears tires screeching. He looks to his left. He sees a truck bearing down at him. He doesn't remember any of its features after that. He begins to act instinctively. He turns his head right. He steps on the gas pedal. The sound of the horn and the tires stops after that. George feels he might escape being hit. He begins to feel relieved. He begins to feel he's always lucky at truly difficult moments. He then feels his car being hit. It's hit on the left rear side. The impact doesn't seem very strong. The car turns counterclockwise however. It also seems to tip a little to the right. George feels his head hitting the roof. He feels a slight pain on the top of his head. He's undergoing hair transplants. He's had the first session twelve days ago. The transplants haven't healed completely yet. There are still scabs on them. The transplanted area is on the top of George's head. George becomes concerned about his transplants. He feels something flowing down his forehead. Shortly thereafter he feels liquid gathering in his eyebrows. Shortly thereafter he also feels something tickling the tip of his nose. He notices a dark streak on the right side of his nose. The streak looks black. George assumes the streak is blood. Shortly thereafter he feels blood flowing off his eyebrows into his eyes. The blood impairs his vision. The blood now definitely looks black. George is surprised at its color. He was expecting the blood to be red. He ascribes the color of the blood to it being dark outside and his being inside the car. He becomes aware of the temperature of the blood on his face. The blood feels cool. George is also surprised at this. He was expecting the blood to be very warm. He doesn't know what to ascribe its temperature to. He begins to think more about the blood. He feels it's very viscous. It doesn't seem to spread much over his face. The blood therefore seems very heavy to George. It seems like a black satin handkerchief lying on his forehead and sliding down. The handkerchief seems to have slid down partly over his eyes and also to the tip of his nose. While thinking about the blood George looks out the windshield. He sees his car turning counterclockwise. It also continues moving forward. There's a truck stopped in the inside left lane of Fourteenth Street. The truck is very large. It's a trailer truck. George's car bears down at the truck. George steps on the brake. He holds the steering wheel firmly. He turns it clockwise. The car continues turning counterclockwise however. It stops a few feet away from the trailer truck. George's nose tickles from the blood. George instinctively wipes the tip of his nose with his left hand. He looks at his hand. It's smeared with blood. The blood looks a little lighter than the blood on George's nose and eyelids. George is angry. He was going to meet Khrystya and a Brazilian movie maker at a restaurant. The restaurant is San Miguel's Mexican Gardens. George feels now he won't be able to meet the two people. He curses. He's still hoping however to meet the two people. He feels blood dripping off his nose onto his chest. He doesn't want his clothes to be bloodstained. This is primarily so because of his wanting to meet the two people. George also doesn't want his clothes to be bloodstained for the normal reason. He decides to get out of the car. He turns off the engine. He takes the keys out of the lock. He puts them in his right pants pocket. He forgets where he's putting them. He opens the door. He gets out. He leaves the door open. He bends forward a little. He lets the blood drip off his face onto the pavement. He looks at the left side of his car. The side is dented above the left rear wheel. The dent is large. It's deep. The metal is broken through in one place. George begins to walk. He doesn't know where he's going. He tries to look up from under his eyebrows while doing this. He has trouble seeing a little because of the blood on his eyebrows and upper eyelids. He sees the truck that hit him. It's parked on the left side of the second road past Fourteenth Street. The truck is quite large. George notices a man before him. The man is black. He looks fairly young. He's a little shorter than George. The man says George wasn't supposed to make the turn. George feels angry. He shouts back at the man. George says this isn't so. He says there's no sign forbidding a left turn. He says the light was green his way. The man says the light was green his way too. He says one isn't supposed to make a left turn from a right lane. George realizes the two streets could be regarded as one. He realizes he would be in the wrong then. He's afraid this is so. He decides not to let the man see this however. George also tries to pretend a little this isn't necessarily so. He repeats there's no sign forbidding a left turn. He doesn't want to talk any longer. He doesn't feel strong enough to pretend he's in the right. He turns away from the man. George walks away from the man. George begins to walk back and forth. He doesn't follow a definite pattern. He behaves as if trying to tramp down fresh snow or tall grass in a fairly small area. He's still bending forward while walking. He tries to wipe off his face with his left hand at one point. He realizes he can't do it properly. He realizes he's merely smearing the blood over his face. He sticks his left hand in his pants pocket. He does this with his hand closed. He's hoping not to stain his pants with blood this way. He's successful in this. There's a handkerchief in the pocket. George takes out the handkerchief. It's of very good quality. The handkerchief is mostly white. There are three stripes along each of its edges. The stripes are about a quarter of an inch wide. They're about half an inch apart. They're dark red. The red is darker than the red of the boots. The handkerchief is Dutch. It was given to George as a gift in Spain at the same time and by the same person as the belt. George begins wiping the blood off his forehead. He realizes he's staining the handkerchief. He remembers its being of very good quality. He feels he shouldn't stain the handkerchief. He takes it away from his forehead. He looks at the handkerchief. It's badly stained. George is sorry to see this. He balls the handkerchief up. He puts it back in his pants pocket. He proceeds walking. He notices another man close to him. The man looks in his fifties. He's white. He's short. He's pudgy. He tells George to move his car off the road. George ignores the man. George feels he doesn't have to worry about his car blocking the road after his being hurt so badly. He's disappointed with the two men not having expressed compassion for him bleeding. He's also disappointed with other people not having expressed any interest in him. He's thinking in particular of the driver of the trailer truck. Shortly thereafter George decides to move his car. He feels guilty about it blocking the road. He also doesn't want his car to be hit by another car. He looks at the street. He's surprised not to see any cars waiting to cross the street being blocked by his car. He concludes they must have been somehow managing to get around his car. He decides to move it however. He goes to it. He gets inside it. He shuts the door. He isn't sure where his keys are. He feels for them in the ignition lock. He then starts going through his pockets. He finally finds the keys. He takes them out. He sticks the ignition key in the lock. He starts the car. He wonders whether it'll drive. He begins to back up. The car moves. George can feel the tire scraping on the bent fender. He proceeds driving however. He moves the car forward. He parks it along the curb on the right side of Fourteenth Street. He turns the engine off. He takes the keys out of the lock. He puts them in the same pocket. He makes a mental note to remember their location. He gets out of the car. He shuts the door. He looks at the damaged side again. The chrome strip along the left rear fender is detached up front. The chrome strip is bent. It sticks away from the car. The strip sticks away about a foot. George wants to look from close up at the damage done to the car. He has to keep clear of the strip. He doesn't like this. At first he wants to bend the strip back in place. He then realizes it won't be possible. He realizes the strip will go on sticking away from the body of the car. He decides to tear off the strip. He does this. The strip comes off easily. George feels slightly sad at tearing it off. He feels he's acknowledging the fact that the car is damaged. He'd rather not do this. He suppresses the feeling however. He tells himself he should be realistic. At first he also plans to save the strip. He hopes it could be put back on the car. He then realizes the strip is damaged too much. He also feels the car is so badly damaged the difference of the price of the strip would be insignificant. He therefore throws the strip away. He throws it close to the curb. He doesn't look where the strip falls. He looks at the damaged fender. It doesn't seem to touch the tire. George sticks his fingers in between the fender and the tire. His fingers fit in there.

George feels however the fender may be touching the tire somewhere else. He therefore decides to pull the fender back. He's afraid he won't be able to do it. He's afraid the metal is too thick. He pulls on the fender. It yields very easily however. It seems very thin. George is disappointed by this. He notices the side of the car is pushed in so that there's a hole between it and the rear window. He walks away from the car. He gets up on the sidewalk. He proceeds walking back and forth again. The blood is still dripping off his face. George has forgotten to bend forward this time. His jacket is open. George notices a drop of blood falling on the inside of the right side of his jacket. He decides to take his jacket off. He does this. He goes up to the car. He puts the jacket on top of the hood. He turns around. He begins walking. He looks ahead. He sees again the truck that hit him. He remembers he should write down the information about the truck. He turns around. He goes to his jacket. He has a memo pad and a ball-point pen in one of the breast pockets of his jacket. He gets the memo pad and the ball-point pen. He turns around again. He walks to the truck. It has a license plate on the back. George can't find the license plate. He's a little surprised by this. He isn't surprised by this enough however to look for the license plate more carefully. He walks to the front of the truck. He looks at the license plate there. The plate is New York State. The number is 803.179. George writes it down. He gets up on the sidewalk again. The black man is there. George asks the man for the man's driver's license. The man gives it to George. The man does this silently. His name is Isaac Robinson. His address is 553 East 108th Street. George writes the name and address down. He begins to look for the man's driver's number. He's not sure where it is. He sees the number R10507549746. He thinks this may be the driver's number. He writes the number down. He isn't sure this is the correct number. He also sees the number 213299-46. He thinks this number probably isn't the driver's number. He remembers driver's numbers are very long. He therefore thinks the first number is more likely to be the driver's number. He decides to write down the other number anyway. He wants to be sure. He writes down the number. At this point the second man appears in front of George. The man asks for George's registration. George is surprised by this at first. This is because of his being hurt. George suppresses his feeling however. He realizes the man has the right to ask for his registration. George gets out his wallet. He gets out the registration. He makes sure it's the registration and not the driver's license. He gives the registration to the man. George then realizes the man must be connected in some way with the truck. George assumes the man must have ridden with the driver in the truck. George realizes he hasn't written down all the important information about the truck. He decides to do this. He decides to ask the man for the registration of the truck. George is pleased to do this. He feels this will compensate for the man's having asked for his registration. He asks the man for the registration of the truck. The man takes out his wallet. He opens it. He gets out the registration. He hands it to George. George looks at it. The name on the registration is Sardo Motor Transports. The address of the concern is 516 West 29th Street. George realizes the man looks Italian. The name on the registration sounds Italian to George. He therefore concludes the man is the owner of the concern. George concludes the man's name is Sardo. He faces in the same direction as the truck. There's a car parked ahead of the truck. The car is large. It's fairly old. It's black. The driver's door in the car is open. The second man goes to the car. He gets inside. He begins writing down the information from George's registration card. George realizes the man must have driven in the car. George realizes this is the reason for the man's appearing at the scene of the accident later than the driver. George assumes the car must have driven fairly close to the truck. He realizes the car could have preceded or followed the truck. He assumes the car had followed the truck. He goes to his car. He stands by it. He proceeds writing down the information from the registration. He writes down the name of the concern, address, and expiration date. He looks for the registration number. He wants to check if the number is the same as on the license plate. He can't find the number however. He decides not to worry about it. He doesn't feel this is important. He remembers about the vehicle identification number. He knows the number is important. He feels he should have it. He feels it's more important than the registration number. He looks for the number. He sees a number. This number is 1965579. George is not sure this is the vehicle identification number. He writes down the number anyway. He then notices another number. It's 1581938393. George remembers vehicle identification numbers also tend to be very long. He suspects this is the vehicle identification number. He writes the number down. In the meantime the second man appears again. He asks George for George's driver's license. George is angry. He feels he's already given the license to the man. George tells the man this. The man says George has merely given him his registration. The man gives the registration back to George. George takes the registration. He realizes the man is right. George doesn't acknowledge this however. He keeps silent. He takes out his wallet. He puts the registration back in the wallet. He gets out his driver's license. He gives his driver's license, that of the truck driver and the registration of the truck to the man. George wants to ask the man for the man's driver's license. George nearly does this. He then realizes there's no need or justification for him to do this. He again keeps silent. The man takes the documents. He turns away. He heads for his car again. George turns right. He walks to the edge of the curb. There's another car parked there. It's a Volkswagen sedan. It's fairly new. It's red. Its right window is rolled down. There's a man inside the car. He's leaning toward the right window. He's looking at George. The man asks if George wants to go to a hospital. George answers in the negative. He turns partially away from the car. He begins to move away from it. He doesn't move very fast. It also isn't clear he's going away from the car. He's behaving this way in order not to appear impolite. The man leans back. The car drives away. George isn't feeling better because of the man's offer. He feels he should. He's surprised at his not feeling better. He turns around on seeing the car drive away. He heads back to his car. There's a man standing next to George's car. He looks in his early twenties. He's very tall. He asks George if George wants to have his car towed away. George notices a tow truck on the other side of Fourteenth Street. The truck looks brand new. It's shiny. It's yellow. It's parked along the curb. George assumes the man is the driver of the truck. George also answers the man in the negative. George is angered by the man's question. George doesn't show his emotion however. The man doesn't go away on George's answering him. He stays around George's car. He walks around in one place. George also walks around near his car. He feels the blood having dried on his face. The blood prickles his face. The blood does this like a crown of thorns. The blood especially prickles George's eyelids. George can't open them completely. At this point the second man appears again. He hands George's license back to George. George puts it away. The man looks at George's head. He asks George if George wants to go to a hospital. George ignores the question. He's reminded of his injury. He's again concerned about the state of his transplants. He's facing the man. George bends his head down. This way the man can see the top of George's head. George asks the man if he's still bleeding. The man looks at the top of George's head. He says he can't tell. He says there's no blood flowing however. George realizes the inconsistency of the man's answer. He's angered by the answer. He lifts his head. He shifts his eyes right in the process. He sees a police car arrive at that moment. The police car stops between George's car and the truck. The police car stops at an angle of about forty-five degrees to the corner of the sidewalk. The police car faces in the same direction as the truck. The police car is black. There are two policemen in it. They get out. They're in their late twenties. The policemen are about the same height as George. They get up on the sidewalk. The black man is standing there. He walks toward the policemen. So does George. So does the second man. One of the policemen asks what'd happened. George explains. The other two men are silent. They apparently agree with George's explanation. The policeman asks where George's car is. George points it out. They all walk to it. They look at it. The man from the tow truck has joined the group. They get back up on the sidewalk. The other policeman asks George and the other men for their driver's licenses and registrations. George gets his registration and driver's license out of the wallet. He gives them to the policeman. The other policeman looks at George. The policeman asks if George wants to go to a hospital. George says he doesn't know. He remembers Khrystya. He says he'll call someone first. There's a gas station on the other side of Fourteenth Street. There's a phone booth outside the station. George looks in the direction of the station. He sees the phone booth. He says he'll call from the station. He points at it while speaking. He heads for it. He puts his wallet, memo pad, and ball-point pen in his rear pants pocket. He looks around before crossing the street. There's no traffic in the street. George crosses the street. He goes to the phone booth. He wonders if there'll be a phone book there. He gets to the phone booth. There is a phone book there. George is relieved to see it. He looks up the number of San Miguel's Mexican Gardens. He's afraid he won't remember the number. He feels this because of the accident. He keeps the book open. He lifts the receiver. He deposits a dime in the phone. He dials the number. He remembers it. He's indifferent to this. The phone rings twice. A male voice answers. George recognizes the man as the manager of the restaurant. George had spoken to the man during his previous visit to the restaurant. The man is Mexican. George speaks Spanish. He'd spoken Spanish with the man. George doesn't feel like doing this now. He feels too tired. He hopes the man won't recognize him. George says he was supposed to meet a girl in the restaurant. He says her name is Khrystya. He asks the man to call Khrystya to the phone. George is afraid the man won't identify her readily. There's a silence on the other end of the line. George says hello. No one answers. George is prepared to wait a long time. After a few seconds however a female voice says hello. George asks if it's Khrystya. The voice says it is. George then explains what'd happened. Khrystya says it's terrible. George then asks Khrystya to come to the scene of the accident in a taxi. He says it's on Fourteenth Street and the West Side Highway. He's afraid this may not be a precise enough description. He says there's a gas station there. There's a sign on a post next to Fourteenth Street at the gas station. The sign is large. It's round. It's orange. It looks like a moon low over the horizon. The sign says "GULF." George sees the sign. He says the station is a Gulf station. Khrystya says she'll be there right away. George remembers the Brazilian movie maker. He asks about him. Khrystya says the movie maker couldn't make it. George is relieved. He's also disappointed. George and Khrystya hang up. He goes back to the scene of the accident. He crosses the street. He gets up on the sidewalk. The black and second man are standing there. The second man again asks George if he wants to go to a hospital. George says he does. He says he'll wait for someone however. He asks the man if he'll take him to a hospital. The man laughs. He says he can't. He says he has to be on the Island that night. George gets angry. He says so does he. He curses. He feels ashamed of this. He explains to the two men he's not cursing them but his luck. He says he had an important appointment that night. By this he means the appointment with the movie maker. George says this in spite of the movie maker not having showed up. George remembers his head again. He bends it down. He asks if it's bleeding. The two men look at the top of George's head. They say they can't tell. The black man says it looks as though George had hit a grid iron. The second man says George must have hit the mirror. The black man says George must have grazed his head on the roof. George lifts his head. He's very worried about his hair transplants. He decides to confide in the men. He tells them about the hair transplants. He asks if the transplants look all right. He again bends his head down. The men look at the top of his head again. They say they can't tell. They say George's scalp is all covered with blood. The second man says he can see the plugs however. George asks the man if they're in. The man says he doesn't know. George feels depressed. He's reminded of the blood on his face. He turns around. He notices the policemen in their car. One of them is filling out a form. George goes up to the police car. He tells the policemen he'll go over to the gas station. He says he'll wash off his face. He says if a girl comes looking for him to tell her he's there. The policemen agree to this. George gets off the sidewalk. He looks around again. There's no traffic again. George crosses the street. He walks to the gas station. There's a teenager sitting outside the station. He sits on a soft-drink box. He's leaning against the wall. The box rests on its narrower edge. The garage door is open. The teenager sits next to it.

He looks Latin American. George goes up to him. George asks for the men's room. The teenager points inside the garage. He says the men's room is on the right. He has no accent. This doesn't change George's opinion about the teenager's ethnic background. George walks inside the garage. He looks to the right. He sees a door in the far corner. He goes to the door. He opens it. The door does lead to the men's room. The men's room is very small. There's a toilet, sink and towel dispenser there. The toilet is on the left of the door. The sink is in the far right corner in respect to the door. The towel dispenser is on the wall on the right above the sink. The dispenser is on the level of the head of an average-height man. There's a mirror in the front of the dispenser. The men's room is white. So are all the fixtures. The men's room is dirty. Its floor is a little higher than in the garage. George goes into the men's room. He closes the door. He tries to lock it. There's no lock on it. George goes up to the sink. He looks in the mirror. There isn't as much blood on his face as he'd imagined. There's a wide strip of blood running down the middle of his forehead. The strip is the widest at the eyebrows. They're caked with blood. It covers George's upper eyelids. It then runs down the right side of his nose. There's blood inside his right nostril. There's no blood between the nostril and the edge of the mouth. The chin below the right corner of the mouth is also covered with blood. The blood is brown. George's face looks part Negro and part white. George bends his head down. He looks in the mirror from under his eyebrows. He looks at the top of his head. It's covered with blood. The little hairs of the transplants are sticking out from under the blood. George can't tell whether the plugs have been damaged or not. The blood looks largely red. It seems the plugs are still bleeding. George resigns himself to this. He decides not to worry. He turns to the sink. He turns on the hot water faucet. No water comes out. George turns on the cold water faucet. The water comes out. George scoops some water up in his right hand. He turns to the mirror. He washes his forehead. He then turns back to the sink. He scoops up more water. He proceeds washing like this. His eyebrows are very thick. A lot of blood has collected in them. George has to wash them for a long time. He has to squeeze the blood out of them. They feel slimy then. They feel like leeches. On washing the blood out of his nostril George wonders if the blood had come from his head or the inside of the nose. He's not sure of the answer. He feels the first explanation is the more probable. This is so because of his nose not hurting. George wonders how the blood has gotten down to his chin without flowing past the corner of his mouth. He can't find an explanation for this. While washing the blood off his hands he sees it on the background of the sink. The blood looks brown then. It looks like rust dissolved in water. The blood also looks like menstrual blood. George is careful not to wash his scalp. He doesn't want to loosen up the blood around the transplants. He's noticed there are no towels in the dispenser. He decides to dry his face with his handkerchief. He gets the handkerchief out. He looks at it. It's stained solid with blood only in one of the corners. The handkerchief is stained with blood only here and there on the rest of its surface. George is careful to wipe his face off with the clean part of the handkerchief. He puts the handkerchief in his pocket after drying his face. He happens to look down on his pants. He notices there are a few blood stains on the inside of his right thigh. They aren't very big. George feels indifferent about them. He goes out of the men's room. He shuts the door. He walks out of the garage. He passes by the teenager. The teenager points out the tow truck to George. The teenager says the tow truck can tow George's car away. George keeps silent. He assumes the teenager has an arrangement with the tow truck. George assumes the teenager calls the tow truck when there's an accident nearby. George assumes the teenager gets a kickback for every car towed away. George assumes this is the reason for the tow truck having appeared so soon at the scene of the accident. He goes back to the scene of the accident. He again looks around before crossing the street. There's again no traffic in it. George crosses the street. He gets up on the sidewalk. He goes to the hood of his car. He gets his jacket. He puts it on. He walks away from the car. He notices the black man and the second man standing by the truck. They seem to be talking to each other. George goes up to the police car. The policeman is still filling out the report. George asks if the accident was due to his fault. The policeman looks at him. The policeman not filling out the report says it probably was. George then states the reason for his having made the turn onto Fourteenth Street. The other policeman then says the fault probably lies with both George and the truck driver. George asks if he'll lose his license. The policeman laughs. He says George won't. George is indifferent to this. He turns away from the police car. He walks. He comes to the edge of the sidewalk. He looks in the direction of the tow truck. He sees the tow-truck driver standing there. The man looks even taller than before. George also sees a taxi standing in front of the tow truck. The taxi is also shiny. It also looks brand new. It's also yellow. It looks very much like the tow truck. George explains to himself this was the reason for his not having noticed the taxi right away. He assumes Khrystya has come in the taxi. He wonders how long the taxi has been standing there. He's concerned about Khrystya having gone away without having found him. He then notices however one of the taxi doors being open. It's the right rear door. George therefore assumes the taxi has just arrived. He notices a girl getting out the door. She remains partly hidden by the taxi. George notices she's slender. He notices she's not very tall. He notices her hair is loose. He notices the hair is light brown. The girl looks like Khrystya to him. He assumes the girl is Khrystya. She's wearing a pants suit. The suit is of a casual cut. The jacket of the suit is of the Eisenhower type. The suit is white. George has never seen it on Khrystya. He continues assuming the girl is Khrystya. He prepares himself to cross the street. He again looks around. There's no traffic again. George crosses the street. He heads for the taxi. The girl closes its door. She heads toward George. He now sees she's Khrystya. He sees now she's carrying a bag in her right hand. The bag is very large. It's flat. It's woven from reeds. It looks like a shopping bag from one of the Latin countries. George notices Khrystya is wearing a shirt under the jacket. The shirt looks like a man's shirt. It's checkered. The colors are red, green, and black. George also notices Khrystya is wearing low-heeled shoes. They're beige. George and Khrystya meet about five feet in front of the taxi. He lifts his hands. He puts them on Khrystya's shoulders. He draws her toward himself. He says he's glad she's come. He bends his head down. He presses his lips against Khrystya's. He pushes with his tongue against the inside of his lips. They part. George pushes with his tongue against Khrystya's lips. They also part. They don't part as much as George's however. George is pleased by the lips parting. He was hoping to kiss Khrystya in this fashion. He was expecting her to react in this fashion. He'd kissed her only once before. That kiss had been a very chaste one however. It'd been merely a good-bye kiss. This'd happened three days ago. This was the first time George and Khrystya had gone out together.

EDDIE'S BAR

The bar is actually called Neir's Bar. George says this is so because it's only near Eddie's Bar. He says the real Eddie's Bar doesn't exist. It's as if he felt Eddie's Bar is an ideal concept. He and Khrystya call the bar Eddie's because of the following incident. This'd happened the first time they were at the bar. They'd been sitting at a table. They'd been at the bar for over an hour. There was a man sitting at the bar. He was in his late sixties. He was drinking heavily. He was drunk at this point. He got up from the bar. He was apparently ready to leave. He wanted to go the the bathroom before leaving. He went to the bathroom. It was close to George's and Khrystya's table. The man got out of the bathroom. He stopped at George's and Khrystya's table. He began talking to George and Khrystya. The man's speech was slurred. His words didn't make any sense. The bartender noticed the man. The bartender was apparently the owner of the bar. The man was apparently an old customer. The bartender came over to the man. The bartender put his hands on the man's shoulders. He did this quite brusquely. He drew the man away from the table. The bartender told the man to go home. The bartender also spoke quite brusquely. He addressed the man as Eddie. George and Khrystya told the bartender the man didn't disturb them. The bartender paid no attention to them however. He proceeded to usher the man out of the bar. The man obeyed the bartender. It was as if the bartender were the man's father. The man's behavior was probably due to his being an old customer. The bar consists of three sections. The first section is the section with the bar. One enters the first section from the street. The first section is long. It's about six feet wide not counting the bar and the space behind the bar. There are stools next to the bar. The second section is roughly square. It's large. There are eight tables in the second section. Most of them are large. Most of them are round. Some of them are covered with table cloths. The table cloths are white. The second section also has a pinball machine in it. The machine is old. The second section lies beyond the first section. The bathrooms lie off the second section. The third section is very large. Its length is that of the first two sections combined. The third section is about as wide as the second section. The third section contains a bowling alley. The third section is entered from the second section. The bar is old. Its decor is old-fashioned. The first two sections are well-lit. There's a light only over the bowling lane in the third section. It's warm in the bar. All the stools at the bar are occupied. There are also people standing at the bar. Seven of the tables in the second section are occupied. Most of the occupied tables have more than two people sitting at them. There's no one in the third section. It's Halloween night. It's a little after ten. George and Khrystya are in the bar. They're in the second section. They're sitting at a table. It's in the far left corner of the second section in respect to the front door. The table is one of the round ones. It's large. There's a cloth on it. The cloth is white. Some liquid had been spilled on it. The liquid was probably beer. George had rolled back the cloth. He'd wiped off the table with the dry part of the cloth. The cloth covers about half the table. There's a quarter lying on the cloth-covered part of the table. The quarter lies about in the center of the cloth-covered part. The quarter was there on George's and Khrystya's arriving. The quarter was apparently the tip left by the preceding customers. They were probably the ones who'd spilled the liquid. George had left the quarter in its place on rolling back the cloth. The people at the other occupied tables are young. The people look in their late teens or early twenties. The people drink only beer. It's in pitchers. They're glass. They have fluted sides. At the table closest to George's and Khrystya's there are eight people. They're five men and three girls. One of the men looks very much like one of the girls. This is so in spite of the man and the girl not being brother and sister. The man and the girl obviously go together. The similarity between them lies primarily in their hair. The hair is fairly short. It hangs low on the back of the neck however. The hair is wavy. It's shiny. It's brown. It looks like dark brown liquid stirred up to the point of having waves. The liquid could be black coffee. The couple have a Halloween mask. The mask consists of a pair of eye glasses attached to a nose and a moustache. The glasses are round. Their frame is black. They actually have no lenses. The nose is large. It's hooked. It's plastic. It's orange and red. The moustache is thick. It's stubby. It's black. The man and the girl put the mask on from time to time. The other people at the table usually laugh at the person with the mask on. With the mask on the man and the girl are practically indistinguishable. At least this is what George feels. He and Khrystya drink vodka mixed with water with a twist of lemon peel, a squirt of lemon juice, and ice. The reason for the lemon juice having been put into the drink in addition to the twist of lemon peel is because there's no fresh lemon at the bar. Otherwise the drink would have had a quarter of a lemon twisted into it. The drinks seem weak to George and Khrystya. The drinks seem watered down. George and Khrystya have commented on this. They don't mind this however. This is so because of the drinks' being relatively cheap. They cost sixty cents apiece. George and Khrystya have been paying close to a dollar per drink in other places. Besides, George and Khrystya are in the bar for the atmosphere. They talk while drinking. They talk largely about gay things. At one point George and Khrystya talk about Khrystya's dog. The dog is a bull terrior. It's nearly a year old. The dog is black and white. It's called Bebe. This stands for President Nixon's friend, Bebe Rebozo. George and Khrystya have started talking about the dog because of the dog's being a bull terrier. She says bull terriers are bar dogs. She says they like staying in bars. She says bull terriers are frequently bar mascots. She says she'll have to bring the dog to the bar the next time. At another point George speaks about a woman. He'd met her a few months back. He's seen her once. He's spoken to her on the phone a few times. It doesn't look as though he's going to see her again. This is so in spite of his liking her. The woman's name was Linda Koegler. She was Jewish. She had two sons. They were six and seven years old. The woman was getting divorced at the time of her meeting George. She'd been married eight years. Her husband had had a mistress for the last four years of the marriage. He started behaving paranoid at one point. He left the woman. He moved in with his mistress. He started suing for a divorce. The woman didn't want a divorce at first. On the man's suing, she started suing for a divorce herself however. She didn't live in her home at the time of her meeting George. She lived with different friends. She moved from place to place frequently. She kept her whereabouts a secret. This was due to the following reason. The woman's husband was trying to have a summons for her appearance in court served on her. She didn't want this to happen.

This was due to her suing for a divorce herself. She was suing for a divorce in another county. She felt she'd get a more favorable trial in that county. She tried to have a summons for his appearance in court served on her husband. He also didn't live at his home at the time of her meeting George. This was due to the same reason as in her case. While calling the woman the last time George had learned her summons had been served on her husband. George doesn't know the outcome of the trial. The woman had had meningitis shortly before meeting him. She'd been in a hospital. She'd gotten out of it a few weeks before meeting George. She'd been in it about a month. Luckily she'd come out with no aftereffects. She felt she'd gotten meningitis due to her situation. She'd been told this by her doctors. This was so in spite of meningitis being an infection. This in turn was so due to the woman's resistance having been down as a result of her situation. It was thus easier for her to get the infection. George stresses all this while talking about her. Toward the end of their stay at the bar George and Khrystya read something. They read aloud. They read together. They read in two books. The books are Khrystya's. She's brought them along for George and her to read in. She feels the books are amusing. They're in Ukrainian. The first book is titled *What Kind of People Are There in the World?* The author of the first book is Pidesha. It was published in Jersey City. The first book was published in 1916. The second book is titled *Advice for Those in Love or How to Write Love Letters.* The author of the second book is anonymous. It was published in Winnipeg. The second book was published in 1913. The books are paperbacks. They're in a very bad state of preservation. Their paper has yellowed. It crumbles. Some of the pages in the books have come out. Parts of many pages have been broken off. The books will soon fall apart completely. This was one reason for Khrystya's wanting to show them to George. They're written very clumsily. The language in them is archaic. The spelling in them differs somewhat from contemporary Ukrainian spelling. All this contributes to them being amusing. Among the passages read by George and Khrystya in the first book is the following: "How Do African Negroes Look? 'Negro' means black in Latin. They all have black kinky hair. Their skin however is not black when examined closely. Actually, the blackest people in the world are those of a cross between Negroes and the people of our 'white' Caucasian race, who live in the Sudan. So the scientist Linney was right in saying that when you speak of races don't pay any attention to the color. Negroes' color is yellowish-brown, or dark reddish-brown. The strange thing is that their children at birth are completely white so that they cannot be distinguished from ours. Negroes don't have a beard, or if they do it is very thin. They do have a slight moustache, but in that place on the lip where our moustache stops. Their skull is massive, strong, so that even if you hit a bull with it it wouldn't break. This is so because the bones of their skull have grown together and in ours they haven't. They are terribly tall, being on the average 167-170 cm, i.e. 5 feet 7-9 inches. The front part of their head, that is the face, sticks out, their teeth are strong and large and the lips thick and rolled back. When they are being operated on you don't have to put them to sleep because their nerves are thick, so they hurt less. One of us would scream to high heavens but they don't care. They laugh, joke, or look attentively at their flesh being cut." Among the passages read by George and Khrystya in the second book is the following: "The most difficult thing is to meet a person seen in the street so that one cannot find out the address. It takes great courage to step up to such a person. A woman, obviously, cannot and should not do it. She can at the most induce the man to notice her. But in this she must be very careful not to get herself into some difficulties. During each such meeting it is the best to look the person one wants to meet straight in the eyes. This will cause the man to notice the woman staring. As soon as the man has noticed the staring, the woman can let him understand—through the expression in her eyes or through a motion—that she feels affection for him and would like to meet him. The man should take advantage of this and bravely step up to the woman and introduce himself. After this the woman should smile and be pleasant in her speech and behavior. Conversation should be conducted in such a way as to express everything one wants to say during the first meeting. When a man feels an affection for a woman whom he sees only in the street and has no way of finding out her address, and he would like to meet her face to face, he should also introduce himself in the street since there is no other opportunity. In this he must be very careful because if his behavior is tactless it may give rise to a hatred in the woman and through this he may lose the posibility of her love. Here one should also make the woman understand that one feels affection for her. One can unbeknownst to other passers by smile in a friendly fashion, look inquisitively in the eyes, follow the woman a few times, and, when one knows she will be walking along the street, wait for her. All this should make the woman notice the man. When the woman wants to meet such a man who makes his affection and his desire to meet her known, she should also show through a motion or expression of her eyes her willingness; it is advisable that the woman, seeing the man follow her, take a turn into a less busy street or enter a park and thus give the man an opportunity to step up to her. When the man decides to step up to the woman, he should behave in such a way as not to attract the attention of passers by. He should step up boldly to the woman, bow in a friendly fashion, and ask: 'Will the lady permit me to accompany her on the walk?'—or—'Will the lady permit me to escort her home?' When the woman wants the companionship of such a man she should answer: 'Yes, please.' In the contrary case she should answer: 'Thank you, I don't need a companion.' After a negative answer the man should no longer importune the woman because his persistence will turn the woman even more against him and, if a future opportunity presents itself, he will not be able to meet her. The woman, after her negative answer, should not answer further questions and propositions. At the most she should say: 'Sir, leave me alone.' When the man has received a positive reply he should introduce himself immediately. This is done in the following fashion. One takes off the hat or cap with the left hand, as is done during a greeting, and the right hand one holds ready for a handshake. At this time one should say: 'I would like to ask the lady's permission to introduce myself!' The woman should reply to the bow with a gentle nod of the head and a pleasant smile and extend her right hand for a handshake. At the same time she should say: 'It is a pleasure to meet you, sir.' At this the introduction ceremony is ended." George and Khrystya stay in the bar until shortly before midnight. At this time all the customers at the tables near George and Khrystya are still there. George has been getting the drinks from the bar himself. He's been paying for them while getting them. He therefore doesn't leave a tip. Another reason for his not leaving a tip is because of the table not having been cleaned up on his and Khrystya's sitting down at it. George and Khrystya get up. She was wearing a cape on coming in. The cape has a hood. The cape is fairly short. It's made from a fairly thick material. The material is wool. The cape is lined. The lining is silk. The cape and lining are black. The cape has one button. The button is at the neck. The button is round. It's convex. It's silver. The cape is tailor-made. It was made in New York. The tailor was Ukrainian. George helps Khrystya put the cape on. She puts the hood on. She's brought a handbag along. She takes it. George was wearing a raincoat on coming in. It's of a military cut. The raincoat has a wide collar and lapels. The raincoat has shoulder patches. It has a vent in the back. The raincoat is fairly long. It's made from cotton suede. The material is cocoa-brown. The raincoat has one row of buttons. There are three of them. The raincoat has also one button on each shoulder patch. The buttons are round. They're flat. They have holes in the center. The buttons are metal. They're nearly black. The raincoat was made in France. George bought the raincoat in New York. He puts on the raincoat. He and Khrystya walk to the exit. They pass the bar. The bartender looks at them. They say good night to him. One of the customers says good night to George and Khrystya. George and Khrystya say good night to him. They walk out of the bar. It's in a residential area. The houses are very close together. There are trees along the streets. It's been a warm fall. There are still quite a few leaves on the trees. The streets are dimly lighted. There's a wind. The trees move in the wind. The movements of the branches looks mysterious in the dim light. The movement is like that of people doing something incomprehensible. Quite a few of the leaves are still green. The green color makes the leaves similar to human hair. The hair seems women's. The women seem beautiful. The sky is overcast. It's beginning to rain. The rain is still very faint and fine. The streets form a "T" in front of the bar. The bar is at the junction of the two streets. There are cars parked on both sides of the streets. The cars fill the sides of the streets almost completely. George's car is parked in the street perpendicular to the one with the bar. The car is parked about fifty yards down the street. The car is parked on the left side of the street in respect to the bar. George and Khrystya walk to the car. He walks on her right side. He keeps his left arm around her shoulders. He feels good. He's thinking about the present. At one point he has a recollection however. The recollection is of an incident a few months back. George was in a bathroom. Its floor was covered with tiles. They were small. They were about an inch on each side. The tiles were black and white. They formed a checker-board pattern. George looked at the floor. For an instant it looked normal. George saw the checker-board pattern. Suddenly however this changed. The tiles seemed to have been all shuffled up. It was as if they were loose. It was as if an earthquake had shuffled them up. They seemed to continue moving. It was as if the earthquake were continuing. The lines between the tiles moreover seemed to have become tangible. The lines seemed to be writhing. They seemed to be doing this like worms. Some of the worms seemed chopped up. George had found the experience terrible. He's happy now it's over. The awareness of the experience being over makes him feel almost cozy. It's as if he were lying in a comfortable bed. Feeling Khrystya's body under his arm contributes to this sensation. On coming to within about five yards of the car George stops. He indicates with his left hand for Khrystya to stop. She does this. George indicates with his left hand for her to face him. She also does this. George puts his left arm around her shoulders again. He bends his head toward hers. Khrystya bends her head back a little. The hood on her head slips back a little. While bending his head down George turns it to the right a little. He exposes his left cheek to the rain. He feels the rain fall on his left cheek. The rain feels cool. It feels very pleasant. It feels refreshing. George realizes even more rain must be falling on Khrystya's face. This is so because of the position of her face. George imagines the rain falling on his face to be falling on hers. This is what he retains in his memory of the moment. He presses his lips to Khrystya's. He and Khrystya kiss. Their mouths eventually open. His and her tongues eventually touch. At one point George puts his right hand inside Khrystya's cape. He puts his hand on her breasts. Khrystya is wearing a sweater. It's fairly thin. It's cashmere. Khrystya is wearing a slip under the sweater. She isn't wearing a bra. George doesn't feel the slip. It seems to him Khrystya is naked under the sweater. He feels her breasts. They're fairly small. They're firm. George can't feel the nipples on them. The breasts feel very nice to him. They seem to swirl like eddies on the surface of water. The breasts also seem to be iridescent like oil spills on the surface of water. George seems to feel the iridescent color with his hand. The day had been fairly cold. It'd been gloomy. The sky had been hazy most of the day. George had worked that day. He has a window in his office. The window faces west. George had looked out the window at sunset that day. He'd seen the sun set. There are hills on that part of the horizon. They're overgrown with trees. The trees are leafless now. This is because of George's place of work being further north and in the mountains. George had seen the sun sink behind the trees. It'd been pale. It'd been almost white. It'd seemed cold. It'd also seemed flattened out. Its shape had resembled that of a pig. The sun had seemed an enormous white pig sinking behind the trees. George seemed to have seen the rays of the sun separated from each other. They'd seemed very sparse. They'd seemed short. They'd seemed whitish. They'd seemed the stubble on the skin of the pig. George imagines the sky behind the clouds at this moment. He imagines the sky black. He imagines stars in it. He imagines them large and luminous. He imagines hearing pigs' oinking coming from the stars instead of light. He imagines the smell of pigs and warmth coming out of the sky as if out of a dark pigsty. Both of these images aren't unpleasant.

CINNAMON FLOWER

The name of the restaurant is *FLOR DE LA CANELA*. The name is Spanish. It means CINNAMON FLOWER. The restaurant is Peruvian. It's located in a basement. The restaurant is long. It's narrow. There are tables along the two long walls and the middle of the restaurant. The tables along the walls are located in booths. The bar is in the back of the restaurant. The bar is along the right wall looking in from the entrance. The toilet is opposite the bar. The kitchen is beyond the bar. The door to the kitchen is in the same wall as the bar. The decor in the restaurant is cheap. The furniture is plain. The paintings on the walls are amateurish. The paintings are of Peruvian Indians. The restaurant is brightly lit. The lighting is too strong for a restaurant. This heightens the feeling of cheapness. The restaurant seems a cafeteria. George is in the restaurant. He's alone. There are four other men in the restaurant. They sit at one table. It's in the last booth on the left side of the restaurant looking in from the entrance. The men all look at least partly Indian. George suspects they're all connected with the restaurant. This is so because one of them is the bartender and another the waiter. This is so in addition due to the men's not eating or drinking anything. The men are merely talking. They're laughing frequently. George is sitting in one of the booths on the right side of the restaurant looking in from the entrance. The table in the booth is covered with a table cloth. The table cloth is plastic. It isn't smooth. It has the pattern of a straw mat pressed into it. The table cloth is green. The green is bright. The color looks cheap. It's unpleasant. George hasn't ordered anything to eat or drink. He'd told the waiter he was expecting someone. George had told the waiter he'd order later. George is writing. He's writing on a pad. It's quadrille. It's white. George is writing with a ball-point pen. The ink in it is blue. George has come to the restaurant straight from work. He's brought the pad along. He's brought it in his attache case. The case lies on the seat on his left side. George is writing about the restaurant. He's at the restaurant for the first time. He'd been told about the restaurant. He'd been told its name and location. He'd found the name beautiful. This was the reason for his coming to the restaurant. George had found its decor cheap. In his opinion the decor clashes with the name. This is the reason for his describing the restaurant. He wants to capture the cheapness of the decor. He's meeting Khrystya. It was she who'd told him about the restaurant. She doesn't speak Spanish. She therefore didn't know the meaning of the name of the restaurant. George came to the restaurant about five minutes early. He's been in the restaurant about twenty minutes. He's been writing for about fifteen minutes. He looks at his watch. He's upset about Khrystya's being late. This interferes with his writing. George struggles with it from now on. He stops almost after every sentence. The time between them grows longer. About seven minutes pass this way. At this point George has not been writing for about two minutes. He's sitting straight up. He's staring ahead. He's looking at the outside door. His eyes aren't focused on anything however. He's sucking on the back of the pen. He sees someone enter the restaurant. It's Khrystya. She's wearing a safari suit. The jacket has long sleeves. The suit has pants. It's sand-colored. It's a bit faded. It's been washed a lot. It seems to be of a very good quality. A partial proof of this seems the suit's having been washed a lot. Khrystya wears shoes. They're leather. They have medium-high heels. The shoes have rounded toes. The shoes are brown. Khrystya carries a pouch. It's rectangular. It has a zipper. The pouch is leather. It's brown. It's quite full. Khrystya's face changes on her seeing George. It becomes smoother. This is as prior to the appearance of a smile on a person's lips. A smile doesn't appear on Khrystya's lips however. George's face also becomes smoother on his seeing Khrystya. It relaxes. His whole body relaxes. A smile also doesn't appear on his lips however. George picks up the pad. He turns left. He opens the attache case. He puts the pad and pen inside the case. He closes the case. He looks up. Khrystya has been walking toward him. By then she's come to the table. George gets up. He and Khrystya exchange greetings. She puts the pouch on the seat across the table from him. She apologizes for being late. She says she got delayed. She unbuttons her jacket. She takes it off. George helps her. She wears a sweater under the jacket. The sweater has long sleeves. It's thin. It's synthetic. It's brown. George is left with the jacket in his hands. There are coat trees at the ends of the seats away from the wall. George hangs the jacket up on the tree opposite from his seat. Khrystya sits down on that seat. George goes over to his seat. He sits down on it. He looks at Khrystya. The expression on her face tells him she's ready to order something. He suspects it'll be a drink. He turns around in the direction of the bar. He sees a man walking in his direction. The man is the waiter who'd come up to George earlier. George waits for the waiter to come to him. George turns his head so as to look at the waiter. The waiter has brought two menus. He puts one of them in front of Khrystya and one in front of George. During this George shifts his eyes to Khrystya. He looks her in the eyes. He asks if she wants to have something to drink. She answers in the affirmative. She looks at the waiter. She says she wants vodka mixed with water with a twist of lemon in it. She speaks in English. George shifts his eyes onto the waiter. George repeats Khrystya's order in Spanish. He speaks to the waiter only in Spanish from then on. George says he wants the same. The waiter says he doesn't think they have vodka. He speaks Spanish now and from then on. He says he'll check with the owner. The waiter walks off in the direction of the bar. George and Khrystya exchange a few words. George and Khrystya look at the menus. The menus are in Spanish and English. George decides on potatoes *huancaina* style and steak. The potato dish is called *papa al la huancaina* on the Spanish menu. George decides on the dish because of its Peruvian-sounding name. He'd wanted something Peruvian. The steak is called *bistex* on the Spanish menu. This is true of all steak dishes on the menu. George finds this funny. He's never seen steak called this in Spanish. It's called *bistec* or *biftec*. George assumes *bistex* is either a Peruvian form or a spelling error. The potato dish costs a dollar twenty-five. George feels the price is high. He assumes the dish is good because of that. He asks Khrystya what she'll order. She says it'll be a steak and fried kidney beans. The dish is called *bistex con frijoles* on the Spanish menu. The waiter returns. He carries two glasses. They're fairly tall. They contain liquid. It fills about a quarter of each glass. The liquid is brownish. The waiter smiles. He puts the glasses in front of Khrystya and George. The waiter says he's brought some whiskey. He says they have no vodka. Khrystya protests this. She says she doesn't want any whiskey. She says she and George didn't order whiskey. The waiter repeats they have no vodka. He says George and Khrystya should take the drinks. The waiter says the owner had already poured the drinks. George looks at Khrystya. He grimaces. The grimace expresses his resignation. He says they should try the whiskey. He's hoping they won't be charged for it. He feels they won't. This is the reason for his wanting to try the whiskey. Khrystya appears to have changed her mind. She stops protesting. George looks up at the waiter. George says it's all right. He says they're ready to order. He gives the waiter the order. George asks what *papa a la huancaina* is. The waiter says it's boiled cold potato with a sauce. He says the sauce has eggs, olive oil, and lemon juice in it. He says George will like the dish. George asks if the dish is a typical Peruvian dish. The waiter answers in the affirmative. George is glad at having made the choice. The waiter asks if George and Khrystya want soda with their drinks. George translates the question into English for Khrystya. She answers in the negative. George answers the waiter in the negative. The waiter asks if George and Khrystya want ice with their drinks. George answers in the negative. He then asks Khrystya if she wants ice in her drink. He implies he knows she doesn't. She answers in the negative. George repeats the answer to the waiter. George then remembers wanting a drink with the meal. He asks the waiter if they have beer. The waiter answers in the affirmative. George asks the waiter if they have Peruvian beer. The waiter answers in the negative. George asks what beer they have. The waiter says they have Budweiser. George says he'll have a bottle. He asks Khrystya if she wants a beer. She answers in the negative. George tells the waiter that'll be all. The waiter walks away. George is puzzled by the waiter's having brought the two drinks. He explains to himself again they must be on the house. He's not sure this is so however. He feels uneasy about that. The sensation stays with him until the bill is brought. He and Khrystya start drinking. They talk while drinking. The talk is about nothing in particular. It's impassive. A few minutes after departing the waiter returns. He brings bread, butter, place settings, and napkins. The bread is Italian. The waiter puts everything on the table. He puts everything in its proper place. He leaves after that. George offers Khrystya some bread. She refuses. George takes some bread and butter. He eats while drinking. About five minutes after departing the waiter returns. He brings a glass, a bottle of beer, and a plate with food on it. The food is the potato dish. The plate is small. The dish consists of lettuce, potato, and sauce. The lettuce is laid out on the plate. There's half of a potato. The potato is large. It's boiled. It looks cold. It looks like a person's cold hands. They seem clasped. The potato lies on top of the lettuce. The sauce is fairly thick. It's yellowish. There's a fair amount of it. The sauce partly covers the potato. The sauce looks like mayonnaise. The waiter puts the glass, bottle and plate in front of George. George asks if the dish is *papa a la huancaina.* The waiter answers in the affirmative. He wishes George good appetite. The waiter goes away. George is surprised at the small amount of food. This is due to the relatively high price of the dish. George feels he won't like the dish. This is due to its being so expensive and looking so common. George expresses his disappointment to Khrystya. He's reluctant to eat. He decides he should do it however. He pours himself some beer. He drinks. He starts eating. The sauce tastes like mayonnaise. The sauce tastes very good however. The potato is very smooth. It's almost creamy. It tastes very good. George is surprised at liking the dish. He still feels it's too expensive however. This feeling stays with him. The feeling will mar for him the pleasure of the meal in the future. He and Khrystya talk during his eating. They again talk about nothing in particular. About five minutes after George's finishing eating the waiter arrives with the main courses. He asks who's to get what. George tells the waiter. The waiter puts the proper dishes before George and Khrystya. The waiter picks up the plate from the potato dish. He wishes George and Khrystya good appetite. The waiter goes away. Both the dishes have potato chips with them. George and Khrystya start eating. Both of the steaks are broiled. They're both tough. The potato chips are hard. George and Khrystya talk while eating. They again talk about nothing in particular. They don't talk very much. One thing they talk about is the food. Neither George nor Khrystya like the food very much. He dislikes the food more than she does however. She eats about half of the meat and a third of the beans. About halfway through the meal she suggests George take some of the beans. He likes beans. He takes some. He finds the beans very salty however. He eats only a few forkfuls of them. He leaves the rest on the plate. Toward the end of the meal the owner comes up to George's and Khrystya's table. He looks in his late twenties. He looks Indian. He looks less Indian than the waiter however. The owner is tall. He's about six feet tall. He's slender. He's fairly handsome. He's fairly elegantly dressed. He speaks to George and Khrystya. The owner speaks English. He asks how George and Khrystya like their food. George answers the owner. George speaks Spanish. He says the food is good. He feels there's no point in being critical. He's glad Khrystya doesn't understand Spanish. He feels she would have contradicted him. He feels he wouldn't have said it in English. He and the owner speak Spanish from then on. The owner asks George what nationality he is. George says he's Spanish. The owner apparently believes George. This is so because of George's being fluent and having practically no foreign accent in Spanish. The owner also speaks a little with Khrystya. The owner and Khrystya speak in English. They speak about Peru. They speak about the political and economic situation in Peru. This is due to Khrystya's having spent some time in Latin America. Khrystya poses the owner a few questions. He stays about five minutes at George's and Khrystya's table. He then goes away. While eating, George has the following thoughts. First, he remembers an incident from two years ago. It was late fall. It was early in the morning. It was raining. George was taking his daily run. He was in the woods. He was passing some rocks. They were big. They were about a dozen feet wide. The rocks were partly hidden behind grass and bushes. The rocks were wet from the rain. They were bluish. They shone in the light coming from the sky. They seemed luminous. They seemed human eyes. The eyes seemed those of fanatics. The fanatics seemed religious fanatics. George was reminded of the incident this morning. He was reminded of the incident while running past the rocks. It's also late fall. It was cloudy this morning. It didn't rain however. George was reminded of the incident by his activity, location, and time of the year. Next, George remembers a simile. He'd thought of it a few days ago. It's as follows. Blood in the wound is like a smile on a person's lips. George doesn't remember how he'd thought of the simile. He's reminded of it now by the incident with the rocks. He's reminded of the simile by the simile in the incident. The poetic nature of the first simile makes him think of the second one. While thinking of the second simile he thinks of the phrase "a wound smiles with blood." He plans to use the phrase in his writing some day. He doesn't know how he'll use the phrase. Next, he thinks of the following incident. It took place a few days ago. It was the preceding Saturday. It was in the daytime. George was home. He was alone. He was walking. He was in the sunroom. He was going from the kitchen to the living room. He happened to look at the ceiling above one of the windows. He saw cobwebs hanging there. They were quite long. They were about a foot long. There were quite a few of them. The ceiling and walls in the room are white. The cobwebs looked dark. They were swaying. They made George think of hands. The hands seemed to be waving. They seemed to be waving to George. There was something sad in the act. The sadness was like that at a departure. The sadness seemed to be connected with George's being alone and his house being ill-kept. Seeing the cobwebs George thought of the phrase "in an ill-kept house cobwebs hanging off the ceiling sway like human hands waving good-bye to the owner." He's reminded of this incident by the previous simile. The poetic nature of the previous simile makes him think of the simile in this incident. Next, George thinks of an idea he's had for a long time. The idea is his writing about Leshchenko. George doesn't know what form the writing will take. The facts of Leshchenko's life, as George knows them, are the following. Leshchenko was born in Kiev. He's considered Russian. He was Ukrainian however. This is one of the reasons for George's wanting to write about Leshchenko. He was an officer in the Ukrainian army during World War I. He was a singer. He sang popular songs. He became famous after World War I. He sang then with a Russian emigre band. This was in Paris. One day one of Leshchenko's friends from the army saw Leshchenko performing. The friend came up to him after the performance. The friend asked what he was doing. Leshchenko answered: "As you see, brother, I dressed up as a Russian and am entertaining these silly Frenchmen." He also played the saxophone. He was a hunchback. He was very ugly. He fell in love with a girl. She was very beautiful. She didn't return Leshchenko's love. This was partly due to his deformity and ugliness. As a result Leshchenko committed suicide. He hanged himself. He was a baritone. His voice was beautiful. His singing was very pure. The singing was almost like reciting poetry. One of Leshchenko's best-known songs is *"Akh, eti chornyye glaza."* This means "Oh, these black eyes" in Russian. The song is one of George's favorite songs. George learned all the above-mentioned facts from a friend of his. The friend's name is Bohdan. Bohdan lives in Chicago. He has a tape of *"Akh, eti chornyye glaza."* The recording was made from a short-wave radio broadcast. Bohdan also likes Leshchenko's singing. In describing Leshchenko's deformity he uses the word *"urod."* This means "monster" in Russian. Bohdan uses a Russian word because of Leshchenko's having sung in Russian. In saying this he imitates a hunchback playing a saxophone. George doesn't know why he's thought of Leshchenko at this moment. George wants to speak to Khyrstya about Leshchenko. George wants to tell her about his plan concerning Leshchenko. George is reluctant to do this however. He keeps postponing it. He doesn't know the reason for this. In this fashion he and Khrystya finish eating. At one point the waiter comes up to the table. He asks if George and Khrystya want dessert or beverage. George translates the question for Khrystya into English. Khrystya answers in the negative. George doesn't want anything either. He answers the waiter in the negative. The waiter says it's all right. He goes away. He clearly goes away to prepare the check. Khrystya then gets up. She says she wants to go to the bathroom. George then decides not to speak to her about Leshchenko. George pushes the thought of Leshchenko out of his mind. Khrystya is looking into the depth of the restaurant. She's obviously looking for the toilet. George sees this. He knows the location of the toilet. He doesn't tell it to Khrystya however. He feels she'll find the toilet herself. Very soon she does find it. She picks up her pouch. She says she'll be back soon. She walks off into the depth of the restaurant. George is left alone. He stares ahead. He doesn't think about anything. A few minutes pass this way. The waiter appears. He brings the check. He lays it down before George. The prices of the dishes were fairly low. George therefore had expected the amount on the check to be small. The amount is $16.20. George doesn't believe his eyes. He's upset. He thinks the waiter has brought him somebody else's check. George sees the *huancaina* potato dish, the steak, and the steak and kidney beans written out on the check. He therefore knows the check isn't somebody else's. He thinks the waiter has made a mistake however. George looks at the price of the three above-mentioned dishes. He feels the prices on the check are the same as on the menu. There are two more entries on the check. One of these is beer. The price of the beer is $1.25. George acknowledges having had a beer. He feels the price is a little high. He'd been charged this much at restaurants for imported beer only. He feels he can't do anything about the price however. The other entry is two whiskeys. Their price is $4.00. The whiskeys are spelled out as *"guisqui."* George had never seen whiskey spelled this way in Spanish. He realizes however this would be the closest way of spelling the word in Spanish. He remembers having heard native speakers of Spanish pronouncing the word close to *"guisqui."* He realizes now why. He finds the spelling amusing. He can't feel amused in the situation however. He feels furious. He'd never been charged this much for a drink before. This includes quite expensive restaurants and bars. George feels even more furious because of his and Khrystya's not having ordered the drinks. He has a desire to call the waiter or owner. George wants to tell them the above facts. He's about to do this. He stops himself however. He feels there's no point. He feels he'd be told this is the price of whiskey at the restaurant. He also knows he and Khrystya had consumed the drinks. He resigns himself to the price. He continues being furious however. He checks the addition. The sum of the drinks and food comes out to be $15.00. This figure appears on the check. There's an entry under the above figure. The entry says 8% tax. George remembers having to pay tax. He acknowledges having forgotten about it. The figure for the tax is $1.20. George computes the tax. The figure comes out $1.20. George sees the figure on the check is right. He also sees the final figure is correct. He doesn't have to go through a conscious process of addition. He thus has to admit the figure on the check is correct. He realizes he'll have to pay the figure. This makes him even more furious. He curses the owner and the waiter. George refers to them as "god-damned Indians." He resolves never to come to this restaurant again. He also resolves never to go to another Peruvian restaurant. He also resolves never to go to Peru. He feels better. A thought then crosses his mind. He wonders if the reason for his having been charged so much for the drinks was his calling himself Spanish. He wonders if Peruvians still dislike Spaniards. For a second he thinks this must have been the case. He then feels it couldn't have been. He feels this would have been very unlikely. He feels it doesn't matter anyway. He feels his evening has been spoiled. He's sorry for having come to the restaurant.

LONG FEET/SHORT THUMBS

1. *LONG FEET*

The woman came with the other people. They were three brothers, one of the brothers' wife, and the couple's son. The people decided to go into town. They decided to grab something to eat in town before going away altogether. The woman was going to go away with them. She said she'd stay on the beach however. She asked how long the people would be in town. They answered they'd be there about forty-five minutes. The woman asked how long it'd take to walk from the beach to the house. The people said it'd take about twenty minutes. The woman said she'd stay on the beach another half an hour. She said she'd then walk back to the house. The people agreed to this. They went away. The woman is left alone with George. She's twenty-seven years old. She's about five feet four inches tall. She weighs about one hundred and ten pounds. She's beautiful. Her hair is straight. It's loose. It reaches to about the shoulders. It's blond. It's flaxen. The woman's complexion is very light. Her eyes are blue. They look like the proverbial corn flowers. The woman's nose is straight. It's fairly short. The woman has a faint fuzz growing on her upper lip. The fuzz is fairly dark. This seems strange. The fuzz doesn't make the woman less attractive however. Her upper lip seems a little short. Her upper teeth are a little exposed most of the time. This also doesn't make her less attractive. Her chin is oval. It's strong. This also finally doesn't make the woman less attractive. She's strongly built. Her bust is fairly large. Her hips are fairly narrow. Her buttocks looks strong. So do her legs. The woman wears a bathing suit. It's bikini. It's pink. George and the woman lie about ten feet above the high-tide mark. George and the woman lie with their heads pointing toward the sea. George and the woman lie on their backs. George and the woman lie on separate towels. George and the woman lie about five feet apart. This is so because of one of the people having lain between George and the woman prior to the other people's leaving. Neither George nor the woman had moved after the people left. The woman lies on George's left side. At one point after the other people's leaving George looks to his left. He hasn't spoken to the woman since the people's leaving. He looks at her. He sees the landscape beyond her. It consists of the beach, sea, and sky. The beach is empty. The sea is fairly calm. The sky is clear. The sea and sky are barely distinguishable from each other. George is looking in the direction of Fire Island. He knows this. He feels pain at the realization. He also feels anger. This is due to a recent event in his life. The sun is on his left side. The sun is still quite high. George doesn't see it. He sees it shine on the woman however. Her stomach is flat. It has sunken in a little due to her position. Her hip bones and mound of Venus therefore protrude a little above the stomach. The mound of Venus is clearly delineated under the bathing suit. George imagines the woman naked. He imagines her pubic hair to be golden. He imagines it to be curly. He imagines it sticking up. He imagines it like sun rays showing from behind the mound of Venus. It's as if the mound of Venus were obscuring the sun. It's as if the sun were setting behind the mound of Venus. It's as if the mound of Venus were a mountain. It's also as if the hair were like the sun's corona. It's as if the corona were visible from behind the mound of Venus. It's as if the mound of Venus were the moon. It's af if the sun were eclipsed by the mound of Venus as if by the moon. The eclipse seems full. George will visualize the sun being behind the mound of Venus in his memory of this scene. George and the woman start talking. After a few sentences he moves his towel up closer to her. He lies now about two feet away from her. George and the woman tell each other their stories. She's English. Her father's family is of German origin however. The woman has been in the States about three months. She's been in the States many times before. She comes to the States occasionally to work. She works in the States as a secretary, travel agent, etc. Her profession is public relations however. This is her job in England. The woman is leaving the States in about two weeks. She's going to Barbados. She'll stay there about four weeks. She'll stay there with some friends. She'll then come back to the States. She'll stay in the States about a month then. After that she'll go to Hong Kong. She'll stay there again with some friends. She'll stay there about three months. She'll try working there. It isn't certain whether she'll go to the States or England after that. She's in the process of getting divorced. This is the reason for her travelling. She's trying to rest. She and her husband got separated in February. They'd been married for about a year. They'd gotten married literally weeks after meeting. The woman's friends say the woman had married the man because of her lease having been on the point of running out. She denies this. It's not certain she's right. Her husband was an engineer. He was very dynamic. This was the primary reason for the couple's breaking up. The husband kept changing jobs. The couple had to move many times. They'd bought a house in December of the preceding year. The woman was in the process of fixing up the house. The husband then got a new job. The couple would have had to move. The woman couldn't stand the idea. She decided to leave her husband. She did this. The husband also always lived above his means. At one point the woman asks George about the time. George looks at his watch. About thirty-five minutes have passed since the other people's leaving. George tells the woman the time. She says she has to leave. George says he'll leave too. He and the woman stand up. He's brought a beach robe along. It'd been folded under his head. George shakes the sand out of the beach robe. He puts on the beach robe. George and the woman shake the sand out of their towels. George and the woman fold them. George and the woman do this separately. They then head to the exit from the beach. They continue talking while walking. The beach belongs to a club. George and the woman have to pass the club house on their way out. He's brought his sandals along. They're rubber. They're of the Japanese thong type. George has left them near the club house. He picks them up. He puts them on. George and the woman walk to the house. There's a road leading from the club to the house. The road is perfectly straight. It's perpendicular to the beach. The road is paved with asphalt. At first there's no sidewalk along the road. The woman and George walk along the road. They walk on the left side. There's a bridge about five hundred feet beyond the club house. George and the woman cross the bridge. There's a sidewalk about another five hundred feet beyond the bridge. George and the woman get onto the sidewalk. She's describing to him how she'd met her husband. This'd been in Mexico. The woman and the man had been travelling separately. They met. They travelled together after that. At a particular point the woman describes their stay in

Acapulco. She describes their hotel. It was very expensive. The woman says they couldn't afford it. She says the man lived beyond his means from the beginning. Staying at the hotel the woman and the man had a private bungalow. There was a swimming pool at the hotel. The woman and the man would have cocktails at the pool. There was a band playing at the side of it. George and the woman are walking past a hedge. It's on the left. The hedge is very tall. It's thick. The sidewalk is damaged in that place. There's a depression in the sidewalk. The depression is partly filled out with gravel. The gravel is sharp. The woman is barefoot. She treads carefully over the gravel. She walks slowly. She seems in pain. George notices this. He thinks of offering to carry the woman over the damaged part of the sidewalk. He immediately dismisses the thought as inappropriate however. He then thinks of offering the woman his sandals. He thinks there might be more gravel further on ahead. He asks the woman if she'd like his sandals. She answers in the negative. George looks at her feet while offering her his sandals. There's a break in the hedge at that point. The sunshine is coming from the left. The sunshine is strong. It illuminates the woman's feet very sharply. George sees them very clearly. They strike him as very long. He continues looking at them. With the passage of time they strike him as being progressively longer. Eventually they strike him as being abnormally long. It's as if the woman belonged to another species.

2. *SHORT THUMBS*

Eventually George is to get to know the woman very well. He'll have the following dream about her for instance. He and the woman are about to have intercourse. She lies down on her back. She gets herself ready for the intercourse. This consists of her doing something between her legs. George is already naked. He gets on top of the woman. He faces her. His penis is already erect. George inserts the middle finger of his right hand and his penis inside the woman's vagina. He feels a sharp pain in his finger and penis. The pain is like that from striking something sharp. The pain in the penis is like that of a penis striking teeth during fellatio. George yells. He pulls out his penis. He feels around the vagina with his finger. He finds an object there. He pulls it out. He looks at it. It's a pair of dentures. They're joined together somehow. George is angered by the object. He finds what the woman has done stupid. He speaks to her. He asks why she'd done such a stupid thing. He speaks in an angry tone of voice. He throws the dentures away. The woman is Jewish. She's thirty-four years old. She's five feet two inches tall. She weighs one hundred and two pounds. She's beautiful. Her hair is wavy. It's thick. It's loose. The hair is parted down the middle of the head. The hair reaches to a little below the woman's ears. It's dark brown. It's nearly black. The woman's complexion is light. Her eyebrows are fine. They're plucked just a little. They're black. They aren't painted. The woman's eyes are brown. Her nose is straight. The nose is of medium length and width. The woman's mouth is fairly small. Her lips are full. Her chin is strong. This doesn't detract from her beauty however. Her bust is fairly large. Her hips are fairly wide. Her body looks strong in general. The woman is an experimental psychologist. She's getting her doctorate. She's in the process of writing her thesis. Her thesis has to do with the influence of experience on the mating selection of fruit flies. The woman teaches at a nearby university. It's close to George's house. The woman teaches part time. She teaches a course in experimental psychology. She was married. She's separated from her husband. She's been separated for seven months. She's in the process of getting divorced. She'd been married for nearly fifteen years. Her husband was an interior decorator. He was very engrossed in his work. He didn't devote much attention to the woman. He didn't have a university education. He felt threatened by the woman's getting her doctorate. The woman and man became incompatible. She has two children from the marriage. They're a girl and a boy. The girl is thirteen. She's beautiful. She's small for her age. She seems ten. The boy is twelve. He's handsome. He's also small for his age. He also seems ten. George meets the woman at a party. It is a pre-Halloween party. It's Friday. Haloween is next Wednesday. The woman has come to the party with her children. People had been invited to come dressed to the party as plants or animals. The woman is dressed as a rabbit. She wears a pair of rabbit ears on the back of her head. They're made from satin. They're white. The woman also wears a body stocking. It has long sleeves. It's navy blue. The woman has a rabbit tail attached to her seat. The tail is fairly large. It's round. It's made from cotton. The tail is white. The woman also wears tights under the body stocking. They're black. The woman also finally wears shoes. They're leather. They have very high heels. The heels are thick. The shoes have fairly thick soles. The shoes are black. The woman's daughter is dressed as a cat. She has whiskers attached to her upper lip. They're made from pipe cleaners. The cleaners are white. The daughter also wears a body stocking. It also has long sleeves. It's black. The daughter has a cat's tail attached to her seat. The tail is made from wire and cloth. The cloth is wrapped around the wire. There's a lot of cloth. There are two kinds of cloth. These are black and white. The colors form a spiral pattern. The tail reaches to below the daughter's knees. It's bent a little. It forms a flat letter "S." The daughter also wears tights. They're skin-colored. The daughter also finally wears shoes. They're very similar to those of the woman. They're patent-leather however. They're red. The woman's son is dressed as a rat. He wears a sweat shirt. It's worn-looking. It's gray. The son has a rat's tail attached to his seat. The tail is made from rope and cloth. The cloth is wrapped around the rope. There isn't very much cloth. As a consequence the tail is thin. It's long. It drags on the floor. About a foot of the tail drags on the floor. The tail is also gray. The gray is a little darker than that of the suit however. George and the woman have stayed together practically all the time since meeting. They obviously like each other. They've been talking. They've talked about literature, psychology, and linguistics. In linguistics they've talked about transformational grammar. This is what they're talking about at this point. They're sitting on a sofa. The woman sits on George's left side. She sits in the corner of the sofa. There's a lamp standing on her left side. The lamp has a shade. The shade is hemispherical. It's glass. It's white. The lamp stand is metal. It's chrome-plated. The lamp has three bulbs in it. Two of these are on. They're strong. The light of the lamp is almost literally blinding. This is especially so for someone near the lamp. At one point George glances at the woman's lap. Her hands lie there. George's eyes focus on her hands. Her thumbs are visible. They're thick. They're short. They give the woman's hands a coarse appearance. Their appearance also seems cruel. The woman's hands could be those of a butcher. It's the last joint of the thumbs that's especially short. The tips of the thumbs also seem to have been cut off. They seem to have been cut off by a machine. This is due to both of the thumbs being of equal length and the ends of the thumbs being flat. George visualizes the accident very vividly. He closes his eyes. He grimaces. He almost gives out a yell at imagining the pain. He realizes that there's little chance of the woman's thumbs having been cut off however. This is due to there being no scars at their ends. George assumes the woman's thumbs are naturally short. He assumes it's a hereditary trait. Later on in the evening he happens to have a chance to see the woman's daughter's hands. Her hands are much smaller than the woman's. The daughter's thumbs are proportionally as short as the woman's however. George thus sees his assumption corroborated.

THE CAMELLIA

It was early winter. It was on a weekday. Jim Morrison was going to go to work that day. He'd set the alarm clock for seven. He however woke up before the clock's going off. It was a few minutes before seven. It was light already. It was actually very light. For a few seconds Jim Morrison lay still. He didn't find anything unusual about his surroundings. He then noticed it was very light. He concluded this was the reason for his waking up. He remembered the radio having announced frost the previous evening. He assumed it'd snowed during the night. The room had two windows. The shades on the windows were up. Jim Morrison assumed the lightness was due to the light being reflected off the snow and coming in through the windows. He had a camellia growing on the patio behind his house. The camellia was his favorite plant. Jim Morrison treated the camellia like a person. He considered it a boy. Jim Morrison called it Camy. He associated himself with the camellia. This stemmed from a time about five years before. Jim Morrison was in love with a girl then. She broke off with him one night. It was in the winter. It was the night of a terrible blizzard. Jim Morrison already had the camellia then. There'd been a tremendous amount of snow during the night. The snow had smashed down the camellia. The snow had broken off a good portion of the camellia. The broken-off part was in the center of the camellia. The broken-off part looked like the inside of a person's chest. Jim Morrison saw the damage done to the camellia the next morning. He noticed the similarity of the damaged portion of the camellia to the inside of a person's chest. He felt as if the inside of his chest had been crushed by the events of the previous night. He thus associated himself with the camellia. He felt sympathy for it. He began taking good care of the camellia. He wanted to nurse the camellia back to life. The camellia came back very nicely with time. Jim Morrison also recovered from the experience very nicely with time. He felt he was recovering at about the same rate as the camellia. This further heightened his associating himself with the camellia. The camellia bloomed late in the fall. The camellia had very many blossoms. They'd bloom until the frost killed them. Jim Morrison always wanted to prolong the camellia's blooming. He therefore would cover the camellia up with a blanket whenever there was the possibility of a frost at night. He was interested in a girl at this particular time. He considered himself in love with her. The girl however wasn't responding as nicely to him as he expected. His emotions toward her therefore had begun to wither. Jim Morrison had associated his emotions toward the girl with the blossoms on the camellia. He wanted for the emotions to continue. He therefore especially wanted the camellia to continue blooming. He was therefore very careful to cover it with a blanket the previous evening. He got terrified on realizing it'd snowed during the night. He was afraid the snow was heavy. He was afraid it'd smashed down the camellia under the blanket. He turned cold at this thought. It was as if he too would die if the camellia was smashed down by the snow. He was hoping he was wrong. He jumped out of bed. The camellia could be seen out of the room next to his bedroom. Jim Morrison ran into the room. There was no furniture in it. The furniture had been taken out recently. The room had three windows. The shades on them were down. Jim Morrison ran up to the window closest to the camellia. He raised the shade. The ground was covered with snow. The snow looked heavy. There seemed to be about a foot of it. The snow had given the ground rounded forms. This was where there were plants growing. This part of the ground looked like parts of a woman's body. These could have been breasts, hips, or buttocks for instance. The room was on the second floor. Jim Morrison had to look down to see the camellia. The blanket over it was pink. The blanket was almost completely buried under the snow. The blanket covered a short object. The camellia had been taller than the object. The object was jagged. It could have been a rock for instance. The camellia was obviously smashed down. It looked as if all of its major branches had been broken off. There were branches sticking out from under the blanket here and there. This was along its edges. There were many buds and blossoms on the branches. The tips of the buds were pink. They looked like bruises. The blossoms were also pink. They looked like wounds. There was a sharp point in about the center under the blanket. This could have been seen even through the snow. The sharp point was clearly a large broken-off branch. The branch looked like a human elbow.

DEATH OF A CAT

The cat's name is Choris. This is a corrupt form of the Spanish word *chorizo. Chorizo* means sausage. The corrupt form was invented by two Spanish children replying to their parents' question what is sausage in English. The children had been taking private English lessons. The parents were testing the children's progress in English. They were disappointed with the lack of progress. They laughed at the answer however. The cat is male. It's five and a half years old. It's half Burmese. It's long. It's thin. It's black and white. It's mostly black. It's blind in the left eye. The cat lost the sight of the eye in a fight with another cat. The eye looks nearly normal. Just its pupil is deformed. The eye is also a little cloudy. It's in the winter. It's very cold. It's sunny however. The sunshine is blinding. There's no wind. There's no snow on the ground. The ground is frozen however. The cat is on the patio. The patio is in the back of the house. There's a retaining wall on the side of the patio away from the house. The wall is made of stone. There's a hill above the wall. There are steps going up the hill. The patio is paved with flagstones. They're irregular. There's earth between them. There are practically no plants between them. The patio is empty. There's an unpaved spot in one place on the patio. This is near the steps. The spot is nearly square. It's about a yard on each side. The ground in the spot is all dug up. It looks as though something had been growing there. It looks as though this something had been dug up. This something seems a bush or a small tree. There are many windows in the house looking out onto the patio. They're all closed. The shades on them are down. There's a door leading from the house onto the patio. The door is closed. The house is still. It seems empty. The cat is halfway between the house and the steps. The cat is walking. It's walking toward the steps. There's an orchard on top of the hill. The orchard adjoins the property belonging to the house. The orchard is abandoned. It's overgrown with brush and thorn bushes. The cat is emaciated. It's very weak. It has decided to die. It'll go up the steps. It'll go into the orchard. The cat will wend its way between the brush and thorn bushes. The cat will have to crawl in places. Its fur will get caught on the thorns a few times. Bits of the fur will remain hanging on the thorns. The cat will find a spot under a thorn bush. There'll be leaves on the ground there. The spot will be sheltered by the bush. The cat will feel safe there therefore. The sun will shine on the spot however. The cat will feel warm there therefore. It'll lie down in the spot. The cat will curl up. It'll feel warm. It'll go to sleep. It'll die in its sleep. The cat's body will freeze solid after sundown.

THE FIGURE

George is in his office. He's alone. The door is closed. George sits at his desk. He's very upset. He picks up the phone. He dials a number. He's calling Frank. Frank is George's friend. Frank is in another town. He's also in his office. He picks up the phone. George and Frank talk. George speaks to Frank about being upset. George and Frank talk for about fifteen minutes. There are papers lying on top of George's desk. Among the papers is a writing pad. It's white. It's quadrille. Its top page is blank. There's a pencil lying next to the pad. George picks up the pencil in the middle of the conversation. He draws a figure on the pad. The figure is about a third of the length of the page down from the top. The length of the figure is about two thirds of the width of the page. The width of the figure is about an inch. The figure consists of two angles and two lines. The angles are about the same size. The size of the angles is about sixty degrees. The angles point to the left. They constitute the left and right side of the figure. The two lines are parallel to the top of the page. They're about three quarters of an inch apart. They join the two angles. The figure looks like an arrow with a very wide shaft and a strange end. The figure also looks a little like an unfinished drawing of a room. George isn't aware of drawing the figure. He draws it in about five seconds. He puts away the pencil on finishing drawing the figure. He hangs up the phone on finishing talking with Frank. George gets up from the desk on hanging up. He doesn't look at the pad. He walks out of the office. He goes to the water cooler. He has a drink of water. He goes next to John's office. John is another friend of George's. John is in his office. George and John talk. They also talk about George's being upset. They however also talk about other things. George and John talk for about ten minutes. After talking with John George goes back to his office. George now takes a different route than on going to John's office. The second route is much longer than the first one. The second route is about twice as long as the first one. The second route constitutes the remainder of a circular route George's office is on. George takes the second route in order to give himself time to relax. Walking relaxes him. He comes to his office. He walks in. He goes to his desk. He prepares himself to sit down. He glances at the pad. He notices the figure on the pad. He's surprised at the figure. This is because of his not remembering having drawn it. For an instant George assumes someone had been to his office in the course of his absence. George assumes this person had drawn the figure. This is especially so due to its shape. The shape doesn't belong to one of the types of figures George draws while doodling. He feels he would never draw a figure of this type. He however feels it's very unlikely someone else had drawn the figure. This is so because people seldom do such things in other people's offices. Moreover George has a vague recollection of holding the pencil in his hand while talking with Frank. George therefore concludes he's drawn the figure. He's upset by this. One reason for this is his not remembering drawing the figure. The primary reason for this however is the figure's not belonging to one of the types of figures George draws while doodling. He's frightened. He realizes he doesn't know himself. He realizes he could have done other things without remembering them. He's afraid he might have committed a crime. He feels it could have been a murder. He feels the murdered person would have been a woman. The figure looks to him like a woman's body curled up on the page.

BLACK

The reason for the re-emergence of black in George's life was the re-emergence of the use of black in industrial products. George worked in an office. He held a staff position. It was fairly responsible. George could touch type. He liked to type his rough drafts. The primary reason for this was the illegibility of his handwriting. George had a typewriter in his office. The typewriter was for his own use. George had had the typewriter for a long time. The typewriter had become archaic-looking. This'd been noticed by George's manager. George had been offered a new typewriter. It was black. George had liked black in his youth. Later in his life he'd grown to dislike black however. He had very few black objects in his possession. He found the idea of having a black typewriter revolting. He decided to refuse the typewriter. He said he didn't want it. He was told this was the only typewriter available at this time. He was told it wasn't certain when another typewriter would be available. He was told it wasn't certain the next available typewriter wouldn't be black either. He was told this was so because of black having come into wide use in contemporary industrial products. He then remembered having seen black used in many contemporary industrial products. These were such objects as computers, dictating machines, typewriters, etc. This'd been primarily in ads for the products. George realized the objects had looked nice in the ads. He therefore decided to take the typewriter. He got used to the black in the typewriter very quickly. He grew to like the typewriter. He'd been using an electric shaver. He'd had it for a long time. The shaver had broken a few months after George's having gotten the black typewriter. George had liked the make of the shaver. He decided to buy another shaver of the same make. He however wanted to get a more expensive model. He wanted to buy the shaver as cheaply as possible. He went to a discount store. He inquired about the make of the model of the shaver he wanted. The store carried the model. George was shown the shaver. It was black. George asked if the store carried the shaver in another color. He was told the store didn't. He still hadn't gotten over his disliking black. He therefore decided not to buy the shaver. He said he wanted the shaver in another color. He didn't ask if the model came in another color. He was afraid the answer would be negative. There was a second discount store nearby. George went to the second store. He inquired about the shaver. The store also carried the model of the shaver. George was shown the shaver. It was also black. It was about ten percent more expensive than the shaver in the first store. George now wanted to buy the shaver. He was sure the model of the shaver came in black only. He moreover remembered his new typewriter. He realized he liked its color. He felt this was so because of the typewriter being a machine. He felt the black shaver also looked nice because of being a machine. He however wanted to get the shaver at the cheaper price. He decided to go back to the first store. He asked if the store carried the shaver in another color. He was sure the answer would be negative. He was right in this. He said he wouldn't buy the shaver because of wanting the shaver in another color. He went back to the first store. He bought the shaver. He had a shower curtain in his bathroom. He'd had the curtain for a couple of years. The curtain was plastic. It was largely transparent. There was a design on it. The design was black. The area occupied by it was very small in comparison with the total area of the curtain however. The black in the curtain therefore wasn't noticeable. George was hardly aware of there being any black in the curtain. A few months after his having bought the black shaver one of the loops on the curtain broke. This was due to the plastic having become brittle. George noticed the broken loop. He decided to buy another curtain. He liked the curtain. His bathroom was tiled in green and black. The black also constituted a very small part of the total area of the tiled part of the bathroom. The black in the curtain harmonized nicely with the black in the tiles. George wanted to buy the same kind of curtain. He went to the store he'd bought the curtain at. The store didn't carry this type of curtain any longer. George began to look for the curtain in other stores. He went to three stores. They were all big. None of them carried this type of curtain. George decided this type of curtain was no longer available. He decided to buy another type of curtain. He remembered having seen a curtain in the first store that could have gone well in his bathroom. The curtain was also plastic. The plastic was heavier than that in the original curtain however. The curtain was largely black. It had six transparent circles in it. They were about nine inches in diameter. George decided to buy this curtain. He felt the reason for this was the fact that the original curtain had also some black in it. The real reason for his wanting to buy the curtain however was his having begun to like black again. George bought the curtain. He was afraid the curtain would make the bathroom look too morgue-like. He felt the curtain made the bathroom look very nice however. He felt the curtain made the bathroom look elegant. The transparent circles made him think of the circular mirrors popular in the thirties. A few months after his having bought the curtain the big yearly sales came up. George wanted to buy a few suits. There was an area in the city he bought his clothes at. He went there. He picked out one suit. It was plaid. George didn't see another suit he wanted to buy. The suit needed alterations. It was going to be ready a week later. George agreed to pick up the suit then. He said he'd pick it up in the morning. He came to the store at ten-thirty. It was closed. All the clothing stores in the street were closed. George decided they'd probably open at eleven. He went to a nearby bookstore. He browsed around until eleven. He went back to the store at eleven. It was still closed however. There was another clothing store nearby. George had walked past this store on the way back from the bookstore. He'd noticed the store being open. He went to this store. He looked at the display in the window. There was a suit in the window he liked. The suit was of the unisex type. The suit was knit. It was brown. George decided to buy a suit of this type and color. He went into the store. He went up to a salesman. George said he wanted a suit like the one in the window. The salesman took George to the rack the suits of this type were on. The salesman asked what George's size was. George told the salesman his size. The salesman began looking through the suits on the racks. There were no suits of this type in brown in George's size. The only suit of this type in George's size was black. The salesman told this to George. The salesman took the suit off the rack. He showed the suit to George. George's first reaction was to tell the salesman he didn't want the suit. This was due to the suit's being black. George then realized he liked black now. He remembered the three black objects he'd gotten recently. He actually became glad the only suit of this type in his size was black. He thought the suit looked very elegant. He decided to take it. He tried it on. He liked it. He bought it. This particular night he's going to see his girl. The primary reason for this is her parents visiting her. George hasn't met her parents. His girl wants him to meet them. He puts on a pair of undershorts. They're of the bikini type. Their material is knitted. It's synthetic. The shorts are red. They were made in America. George bought them about six months back. He bought the shorts in America. He next puts on a shirt. It has a wide collar. The shirt has long sleeves. It has three buttons on each cuff. The shirt is body-contoured. It's made from a thin material. The material is sheer. It's synthetic. It's flowered. The flowers are large. The colors in the material are green, yellow, white, black and purple. The shirt was made in Italy. The shirt was bought in America. The shirt was given to George as a birthday present five years ago. He next puts on a tie. It's wide. It's made from a synthetic material. The tie is heavy. It's purple. The purple is very close to that in the shirt. The tie was made in Italy. The tie was bought in America. The tie was given as a birthday present to George about two years ago. He next puts on the pants of the black suit described above. They have an elastic waistband. They don't need a belt. The waistband is joined up front. The pants have only one pocket. It's just below the waistband on the left front side. The pocket has a flap over it. The pocket is very small. A wallet wouldn't fit in it for instance. The pants have a zipper up front. Their legs are wide. The legs have no cuffs. George next puts on a pair of socks. They're woolen. They're black. George hadn't stopped wearing black socks on starting to dislike black. The black of the socks he'd buy didn't use to bother him. The socks were made in America. George bought them in America. He bought them about two years ago. He next puts on a pair of shoes. They're of the loafer type. They have round toes. The toes are quite wide. The shoes have buckles. The shoes are black. George also hadn't stopped wearing black shoes on starting to dislike black. This was for the same reason as with socks. The shoes were made in Spain. George bought them in Spain. He bought them about three years ago. He hadn't gotten to wear the shoes very much until now. He'd worn them only twice before. This'd happened within the preceding two weeks. George next puts on the suit jacket. It looks like a shirt. The jacket has one row of buttons. There are five of them. They're round. They're black. The jacket has cuffs on the sleeves. The cuffs button up. The buttons on the cuffs are the same as up front except a little smaller. The jacket has an elastic in the back at the waist. The elastic gathers the jacket in the back. The suit was made in

Italy. George next puts on a raincoat. It's of a military cut. The raincoat has a wide collar and lapels. The raincoat has shoulder patches. It has a vent in the back. The raincoat is fairly long. It's made from cotton suede. The material is cocoa-brown. The raincoat has one row of buttons. There are three of them. The raincoat has also one button on each shoulder patch. The buttons are round. They're flat. They have holes in the center. The buttons are metal. They're nearly black. The raincoat was made in France. George bought the raincoat in a store on the same street as the suit. He bought the raincoat about two years ago. He next puts on a hat. It's of the German hunting type. The hat is velour. It has a tuft of feathers and bristle on the left rear side. The tuft is held together by a coat of arms. The coat of arms is metal. The hat has a band around its base. The band is made from a cord. The hat is yellowish-brown. It was made in America. George bought the hat in America. He bought the hat about five years ago. He next takes a shoulder bag. It's his. It has two pockets on the outside. The bag and the pockets have flaps over them. The bag is leather. It's brown. It was made in Lebanon. George had put most of his personal things he might need in the bag. These are such things as a wallet, handkerchief, keys, etc. George bought the bag in New York. He bought the bag about six months ago. He hangs it on his left shoulder. He's ready to go.

GEORGE

George has a date with Vicki. She's Romanian. She's been in America seven months only. Her English is quite good. It's still imperfect however. This is true grammatically, lexically, and phonetically. Vicki's voice is soft. It's sweet. It's feminine. George and Vicki have been together for about five minutes. Vicki says: "I saw you on Tuesday."

George is surprised by this. He says: "When?" His voice conveys surprise.

Vicki says: "At noon."

George is even more surprised than before. He says: "Where?" His voice conveys surprise even more than before.

Vicki says: "In a gallery . . . on the Madison Avenue."

George is still more surprised than before. He says: "In a gallery on Madison Avenue? . . . But I wasn't in town." His voice now almost conveys anger.

Vicki says: "Yes . . . in a gallery on Madison Avenue on Tuesday . . . . It was a nice day and I decided to go out for lunch. I decided to take some time from work so I took a walk to the Madison Avenue to look at galleries . . . . I saw you in one . . . . I think it was on about Eightieth Street."

George finds the explanation amusing. He says: "But that's impossible . . . . I was at my job Tuesday noon . . . ." His voice now conveys amusement. George is almost smiling.

Vicki says: "No, you were not . . . . You were with a girl . . . ."

George is amused now. He says: "A girl?" He laughs.

Vicki says: "Yes . . . a girl."

George continues being amused. He says: "What was she like?" He smiles.
Vicki says: "Young . . . and blonde . . . very beautiful . . . very slender . . . and tall . . . . Her hair was short but wavy . . . . She had blue eyes and white skin . . . . She wore a dress . . . . You carried her coat . . . . The dress was white with a wide skirt . . . a little transparent . . . . It had blue flowers embroidered on it . . . . You held her hand . . . . You wore your military raincoat and boots . . . . You walked along the wall looking at pictures . . . talking and laughing . . . ."
George imagines the pictures being windows showing beautiful white clouds in a blue sky.

THE END

It was early summer. It was a Sunday. The weather was beautiful. Jim Morrison decided to go to the beach. He went there with his girl. They went in his car. Jim Morrison decided to go to the beach close to noon. He lived more than two hours away from the beach. It was almost three therefore when he and the girl got to the beach. It was fairly cool. The beach stretched for many miles. It wasn't very crowded therefore. Jim Morrison and the girl went off to the right from the entrance to the beach. There were dunes on the beach. Jim Morrison and the girl settled under a dune. There were no people around for about a hundred yards. Jim Morrison and the girl laid out their towels on the sand. Jim Morrison and the girl took off their clothes. Jim Morrison and the girl were already wearing swimming suits under their clothes. Jim Morrison and the girl brought the Sunday paper along. They settled down to reading the paper. It was the girl who was eager to read the paper. Jim Morrison had bought the paper at her request. He merely read to accompany her. He ran every day. He usually ran in the morning. He hadn't run yet that day. This was due to his getting up late and then going to the beach. Jim Morrison read the sports section. He looked for some running news. There weren't any. Jim Morrison missed running. He also felt guilty about not having run yet that day. He'd planned to run later. After reading for about fifteen minutes however he decided to run. He told this to the girl. She agreed to this. Jim Morrison got up. He went over to the girl. He kneeled down beside her. She turned toward him. He kissed her on the lips. He said he'd be back in about an hour and twenty minutes.

Jim Morrison and the girl said good-bye to each other. He then got up. He was wearing his wrist watch. It was a stopwatch. The time was eight after three. Jim Morrison started the watch. Simultaneously with this he started running. He ran in the direction of the sea. He ran very slowly. This was due to his not having warmed up yet and to the sand being soft. Jim Morrison reached the sea. The tide was close to being high. The beach was fairly steep. The sand along this portion of the beach was hard. Jim Morrison turned right on reaching the sea. He speeded up. He found the going much easier than on the soft sand. He felt good. Within a few minutes he was running fairly fast. There was a light breeze blowing his way. The breeze was cooling off his body. Jim Morrison could feel the breeze especially on his chest. The breeze felt very pleasant. Jim Morrison felt as though he'd had a piece of peppermint candy. The sky was a deep blue. There were a few clouds. They were very high. They were of the alto-cumulus type. They stretched for a long distance. They were thin. They were translucent. They were white. The breeze on Jim Morrison's chest and the clouds made Jim Morrison think of an incident. This'd happened the previous fall. Jim Morrison was driving in a car. He was alone. It was at sunset. Jim Morrison had been driving north. He then turned onto a road leading west. He saw a cloud formation ahead. The clouds were also of the alto-cumulus type. They were illuminated by the sun. They were pink along the west edge. They were gray along the east edge. They had roughly the shape of human lungs. The clouds covered practically the whole sky within Jim Morrison's field of vision. They seemed to be high up. They therefore were obviously huge. They seemed the lungs of a giant. The person seemed a giant both physically and spiritually. Jim Morrison was very moved by the sight of the clouds. He felt elated. He'd been thinking about the clouds on and off ever since. He felt elated again on remembering them now. This increased his enjoyment of the run. He was looking forward to the run. He was sorry to think of its ending. The beach was on an island. Jim Morrison knew the island well. It was very long. It was about thirty miles long. Jim Morrison had run practically the whole length of the island in sections on different occasions. The only part he hadn't run along was from the spot where he'd come to with the girl to the tip he was running toward. This distance was about five miles. Jim Morrison knew this. He wanted to run this stretch on this particular day. He was looking forward to covering this stretch. He was looking forward to having run the whole length of the island. The beach was straight. There were very few people on it. The people on the beach were fishermen and strollers. There were no bathers. After running about a mile Jim Morrison had an urge to urinate. There were people about a quarter of a mile in each direction from him. He was ashamed however to urinate within the sight of these people. He turned right. He ran toward the dunes. He stopped on coming close to them. He stopped his watch. He kneeled down. He looked around. He could barely see the people now. He was sure they couldn't see the lower part of his body. He pulled his penis out through the left leg opening of the trunks. He urinated. The urine made a hole in the sand. The urine foamed around the hole. The foam was white. It looked like the petals of a white flower. The hole looked like the center of the flower. The center seemed black. Jim Morrison stopped urinating. Some of the foam remained on the sand. The foam still looked like petals. These petals seemed wilted. There seemed to be few of them. In other words, many of them seemed to have fallen off the flower. Jim Morrison put his penis back in his trunks. He stood up. He started the watch. He again simultaneously started running. He ran toward the sea. He also ran partly in his previous direction. He ran at an angle of about forty-five degrees to the sea. He proceeded to run along the beach in his previous direction on reaching the beach. The beach continued straight for about another three miles. Toward the end of this stretch there were more people on the beach. They were all fishermen. At the end of the straight stretch of the beach there was a breaker. The breaker consisted of boulders. They were big. The breaker stretched about fifty yards into the sea. There were quite a few people there. There were about twenty people. They were also all fishermen. There were a few cars standing on the beach. Most of them were station wagons. Jim Morrison realized the cars belonged to the fishermen. While running to urinate he'd seen tire marks on the beach. He didn't know their origin. Now he realized they must have come from the cars near the breaker. He speeded up on nearing the breaker. He did this because of the people there. He wanted to impress them by his speed. None of them however seemed to pay any attention to him. He was disappointed by this. He was planning to run beyond the breaker. He had to practically stop on coming to it. This was due to its extending onto the sand. Jim Morrison had to run over the boulders. They were higher than the sand. Their hardness also hurt Jim Morrison's feet. Jim Morrison resumed running at his normal speed on crossing the breaker. It was the speed prior to his having speeded up on coming to the breaker. The dunes stopped past the breaker. The beach got low. The tip of the island was about half a mile away. The beach curved to the right at the tip of the island. There was another island about two hundred yards away. The wind got stronger between the two islands. It blew toward the mainland. There was a strong current between the two islands. The water also flowed toward the mainland. The water swirled. Its surface looked like muscles. They seemed flexed. The water made a noise. The noise sometimes sounded like slurping. The two islands seemed lips. The land seemed to be sucking in the water like a thirsty person. There were buoys between the two islands. The buoys were roughly halfway between the two islands. The buoys ran in a roughly straight line. They were red. They bobbed and swayed. There was a bell on one of the buoys. The bell sounded tinny. Its sound was sometimes prevented by the wind from reaching Jim Morrison's ears. The sound of the bell seemed half-erased writing. Jim Morrison couldn't tell which buoy the bell was on. There was something being constructed in the water a little beyond the tip of the island. Pillars were driven into the bottom of the sea. They stuck up above the water. They stuck up some twenty feet. There was a barge tied to the pillars. There was a derrick on it. There was a sign on the derrick. The sign said "FINI BROS." The pillars were metal. They were rusty. The barge was also metal. It was red. It was also rusty in places. The derrick was yellow. The sign was white on a red background. Jim Morrison liked the color combination of the objects. This was especially true of the colors of the objects contrasting with the color of the sky and sea. The sky and sea were almost an identical blue. Jim Morrison was puzzled by the sign.—The first word was obviously a last name. The name seemed Italian to Jim Morrison. It seemed too short however. Jim Morrison felt it should be something like "Finini." He didn't think about the name very long however. He decided it must have been shortened after the family's leaving Italy. The mainland lay about two miles away from the tip of the island. The mainland was flat. It was covered with houses and trees. The foliage of the trees looked black. The houses were mostly white. The air was hazy. The haze was bluish. The details of the mainland were made indistinct by the haze. The mainland seemed to lie behind bluish glass. This seemed especially so because of no noise coming from the mainland. The mainland seemed to lie behind soundproof glass. The beach got perfectly flat at the tip of the island. There were many puddles along the beach. There were also many sand spits. Jim Morrison ran through some of the smaller puddles. He avoided running through some of the bigger ones. At times the portion of the beach he was running on ended in a sand spit. He then had to run through water. At times it got to be quite deep. It'd reach to above Jim Morrison's knees. Jim Morrison would then have to walk. He'd stop the watch for those stretches of time. He ran fairly slowly along this portion of the beach. At one point the beach stopped curving. The beach went on then in an approximately straight line. This was on the side of the island facing the mainland. The beach there was about parallel to the mainland. Jim Morrison ran quite fast along this portion of the beach. About half a mile past where the beach became straight the sandy part stopped. The beach got rocky. The rocks were fairly small. They were usually a couple of feet across. The rocks seemed to have been piled up by people. There didn't seem to be any obvious reason for this having been done. Having reached this point Jim Morrison stopped. He simultaneously stopped his watch. He looked at it. He'd run thirty-three minutes and eleven seconds. He felt he should run more. He felt he should run at least another six minutes and forty-nine seconds. It was almost impossible for him to run on. He could have run above the rocks. The ground there was overgrown with vegetation however. The vegetation was shrubs and tall grass. The ground above the rocks was also uneven. Jim Morrison therefore decided to run up and down the straight portion of the beach. He decided to run there at least another thirteen minutes and thirty-eight seconds. In other words, he decided to run until being at least six minutes and forty-nine seconds past the planned half-point of his run while finding himself at the point where the rocks began. He proceeded running back and forth. He ran at an uneven pace. At times he ran very fast. At those times he ran under a five-minutes-per-mile pace. He ran at this pace for about a quarter of a mile at a time. He'd then jog. He'd run then at about a ten-minutes-per-mile pace. He'd run at this pace for about a hundred yards. He was basically doing interval training. He ran this way for fourteen minutes and six seconds. At this time he was finding himself at the point where the rocks began. He decided to run back. He did this. He felt good. He felt very strong. He proceeded to run at a steady pace. The pace was fairly fast. The pace was about six minutes and thirty seconds per mile. Jim Morrison was now coming across more and deeper puddles than while running in the opposite direction. He ascribed this to the tide having risen. He was right in this. He no longer could run in a straight line. He had to run around most of the puddles. He had to slow down to do this. He didn't like slowing down. He found the progress tedious. He wished he could run as before. He ran this way for about an eighth of a mile. He then saw a sand spit to the right.

The spit was high. It was wide. It looked dry. It seemed to run parallel to the beach. The spit curved. It seemed very long. Jim Morrison couldn't see its end. The spit was about fifty yards from the beach. Jim Morrison decided to get onto the spit. He decided to run along it. He got in the water. He ran for a few steps. The water reached his crotch. Jim Morrison had to stop. He simultaneously stopped his watch. He proceeded to wade. The water reached to above his waist. The current was quite strong. Jim Morrison proceeded moving toward the spit however. He didn't take his eyes off it. The spit protruded like the front of a thigh out of the water. The thigh seemed muscular. It seemed to belong to a runner. Jim Morrison was reminded of his thigh by the spit. This was one reason for his wanting to get onto the spit. The water got shallower again. The current got weaker. Jim Morrison reached the spit. He got out of the water. He started running. He simultaneously started his watch. He started running quite fast. He was running at about a six-minutes-and-thirty-seconds-per-mile pace from the beginning. He felt good again. He was glad for having gotten onto the spit. The sand on it was quite hard. The running was easy. The spit was drawing slightly away from the beach. Jim Morrison noticed this. This frightened him a little. The fear was partly due to his imagining seeing himself from the beach. Jim Morrison realized he must look as if running on water. It was as if he were afraid he'd sink. It was as if he'd sink losing faith in himself being able to run on water. At one point the spit got to be about a hundred yards away from the beach. The beach then seemed to be terribly far away to Jim Morrison. His fear then got to be quite strong. Jim Morrison found the sensation thrilling however. He found it pleasant. He began to smile. He noticed the derrick, barge, pillars, and buoys in the distance. He heard the tolling of the buoy bell. He proceeded running. He began to wish the strip would rejoin the beach soon. He began to be impatient. He ceased smiling. He wanted to reach the beach as soon as possible. He speeded up. He ran at about a six-minutes-per-mile pace. He passed the construction site. The sound of the buoy bell was now quite loud. Jim Morrison was able to see around the tip of the island. He could see the breaker and people around it. The sand spit then stopped. It did this abruptly. Jim Morrison hadn't noticed its end until very close to it. He actually had to run into the water. He stopped. He simultaneously stopped his watch. He turned left. He was about a hundred and twenty yards away from the beach. The distance seemed enormous. To Jim Morrison the beach seemed barely visible. He didn't feel he could swim this far. This was especially because of there being a strong current. The waves were quite high between the spit and the beach. Jim Morrison now realized the strong current at the other end of the spit was an indication of the spit's not rejoining the beach. He saw he should have realized this. He felt stupid. He decided to turn back. He decided to run to a point closer to the beach. He decided to swin over to the beach from that point. He turned left again. He started running again. He also simultaneously started his watch. He was running fast from the beginning. He was running at about a six-minutes-per-mile pace again. He kept looking at the beach while running. He wanted to find as soon as possible a spot where the beach was close enough for him to swim to. As was said, the beach was getting closer. It wasn't getting closer appreciably however. To Jim Morrison, moreover, it didn't seem to be getting closer at all. He reached the other end of the spit. From this point by now the beach was about seventy-five yards away. Jim Morrison stopped. He again simultaneously stopped his watch. His heart sank. The beach here also seemed too far for him to swim to. It actually seemed farther away than at the other end. Moreover, Jim Morrison realized that while trying to swim to the beach here he could more easily be carried into the sound between the island and the mainland. He was terrified. He realized now the sand spit got flooded at high tide. He realized this from the hardness of the sand. The sand had obviously been under water recently. Jim Morrison decided again to run to a point seeming closer to the beach to him than this end of the spit. He felt it might be the other end of the spit. He decided to swim to the beach from there. He turned around. He started running. He ran very fast from the beginning. He ran at about a five-minutes-and-thirty-seconds-per-mile pace. He ran for a few seconds. He realized then he hadn't started his watch. He started it. He then felt it was wrong for him to be timing himself in the present situation. This was because of his feeling his life was in danger. Jim Morrison felt as if it were obscene or sacrilegious for him to be timing himself. He therefore stopped the watch immediately. He continued running at the same pace. He felt as if he were flying. His feet seemed to barely touch the ground. It was as if they were afraid of the ground. It was as if they pretended to be able to fly. It was as if they were trying to make Jim Morrison capable of crossing over to the beach without swimming. He realized he probably looked like a madman to someone on the beach. Jim Morrison felt imprisoned behind the water as if behind bars. They seemed blue. Jim Morrison felt like a caged animal. He hated the water. He also hated himself for having been so stupid. He again saw the derrick, barge, pillars, and buoys. He again heard the sound of the buoy bell. He was reminded of Hemingway's title *For Whom The Bell Tolls*. He realized the bell might be tolling for him. His heart sank again. Jim Morrison then remembered the sign on the derrick. He realized the name sounded like the word for "end" in French. He was surprised at not having noticed it before. He didn't speak Italian. He wondered whether the name meant "end" in Italian. He chased this thought out of his mind however. He felt the name was a bad omen. He felt this was especially so when coupled with the bell. He felt his end may have really come. He felt even worse. He ran on for a little distance. At this point the beach seemed nearer to him than at any point heretofore. This wasn't true however. The beach was about one hundred and ten yards away from here. Jim Morrison decided to swim over to the beach from here. He began to slow down. He beared left. He stopped when the water reached his crotch. He was facing the beach. He looked to his right. He wanted to see if the breaker and people were visible. They weren't visible. Jim Morrison felt completely alone. He remembered his girl. She seemed completely foreign to him. It was as if he'd never known her. It was as if someone had merely told him about her. He became aware of his body. It seemed his only friend. Jim Morrison felt grateful to his body. He felt close to it. He stood for about a second. He then threw himself in the water. He began swimming. The current was strong. It began carrying Jim Morrison to the left from the beginning. He began to swim harder. He wanted to be sure not to be carried into the sound. The wind was strong. It was gusty. At one point it brought the sound of the buoy bell very clear to Jim Morrison's ears. The buoy then seemed directly behind his back. Jim Morrison was again reminded of *For Whom the Bell Tolls* and of the word "Fini." He was annoyed by this. He felt angry at the buoy and the sign as at the water and himself. The waves were getting bigger farther away from the spit. The sky and water were still an almost identical blue. The beach was a thin line. The line was white. It divided the blue area approximately in half. At one point a large wave passed before Jim Morrison's eyes. It obliterated the line of the beach. The sea and sky merged.

A NIGHT IN THE LIFE

The darkness is like an echo behind George. It's night. George has just come home from work. He's in his house. He's in the basement. The basement is dark. George is standing in front of the door leading to the kitchen. He's standing at the top of the staircase. He's holding an attache case, thermos, and plastic bag in his left hand. The thermos is empty. There was tea in it. The bag contains a piece of cheese and some bread. They are left over from George's lunch. George is holding his right hand on the doorknob. He turns the knob. He pushes on it. The door opens. George sees some light. There's a room next to the kitchen. There's a doorway between the room and the kitchen. The room has many windows. A few of them don't have the shades down. The street outside George's house is lit. Some light is coming into the room from the outside. Some of this light comes into the kitchen. The light is like the air one reaches on coming out from a long dive under water. George feels better. He steps up into the kitchen. There's a light switch on the left of the door. George finds the switch with his right hand. He flips the switch. It operates the light on the staircase. The light is at the bottom of the staircase. The light goes on. It illuminates the kitchen a little. The light is yellowish. It makes George think of an orange. There seems to be half of the orange. It seems to have been nearly squeezed dry. The light switch for the light in the kitchen is on George's right. The switch is about in the center of the wall. George walks up to the switch. He flips it on. The light in the kitchen is in the middle of the ceiling. The light is flourescent. It takes the light a few seconds to go on. It seems to hesitate. It's like a person trying to wake up. The flickering of the light is like the blinking of a person's eyes. The light is fairly strong. The kitchen is quite big. The light seems weak therefore. It's white. The floor and fixtures in the kitchen are avocado-green. The light therefore seems greenish. It makes George think of a lemon. There also seems to be half of the lemon. It also seems to have been nearly squeezed dry. It seems in addition to have grown hard with age. There's a cabinet under the switch. George puts the attache case on top of the cabinet. He lays the attache case on its side. There are cabinets along the opposite wall. The sink is in the middle of the wall. The sink separates the cabinets. The stove is on their left. The refrigerator is on their right. George turns around. He walks up to the cabinet on the right of the sink. He stands the thermos on top of the cabinet. He goes to the refrigerator. He opens it. It's quite full. George puts the bag on the top shelf of the refrigerator. This is next to a pile of cheeses. George closes the refrigerator. There's water dripping from the kitchen faucet. George hears this. He turns around. He goes up to the sink. He tightens the cold water valve. This stops the dripping. George goes up to his attache case. He takes it in his left hand. He turns off the light in the kitchen. The kitchen is now illuminated by the light in the basement. George goes up to the switch operating the light. He turns off the light. The kitchen is dark again. George however can see the outlines of the kitchen because of the light coming in from the room next to the kitchen. He turns around. He goes to the room next to the kitchen. The light switch in that room is on the wall on the left. The switch is on the right of the door leading to the rest of the house. George goes to that light switch. He turns it on. The light in the room is on the ceiling in the right side of the room. The light is soft. It's pleasant. There's a thermostat on the left of the door leading to the rest of the house. George goes up to the thermostat. He looks at it. The temperature in the room is fifty-nine degrees Fahrenheit. The thermostat is set to fifty-six degrees. George feels cold. He turns the thermostat up to sixty-five degrees. There's a hallway beyond the door. George enters the hallway. There's a closet and radiator on the left side of the hallway. The closet is closer to the door. The radiator has a cover over it. George lays the attache case on the radiator cover. He's wearing a raincoat. He takes it off. He opens the closet. He hangs up the raincoat on a coat hanger in the closet. He closes the closet. There's a staircase landing on the left beyond the radiator. The staircase leads upstairs. There are two light switches on the wall on the right on the staircase landing. They operate the lights at the bottom and top of the staircase. George goes up to the switches. He turns on the lights. They're fairly strong. They're pleasant. George goes back to the room off the kitchen. He turns off the light there. He turns around. He goes to his attache case. He picks it up. He steps up onto the staircase landing. He climbs the stairs. The stairs creak under his feet. The sound is pleasant. It's reminiscent of that of a harpsichord. There are three doors at the top of the staircase. The doors on the left and right lead to rooms. These doors are open. The door in the middle leads to a bathroom. This door is closed. The room on the left if nearly empty. The room on the right has a credenza, cot, two chairs, table, free-standing cabinet, lamp, and bookcase. The room is George's study. George goes into the room. He lays his attache case on the cot. He goes back into the hallway off the staircase. He goes into the bathroom. He leaves the door open. It's therefore light in the bathroom. George wears contact lenses. He takes the contact-lens case out of his pants pocket. He puts the case on the sink. He walks out of the bathroom. He closes the door. He walks down the hallway. This is away from the staircase landing. There are also three doors at this end of the hallway. The hallway makes a turn to the right at the end. Two of the doors are there. One of them faces away from George. This door leads up to the attic. The other one is opposite the attic door. This door leads to George's bedroom. The third door is directly opposite George. This door leads to an empty room. George can see the room is empty in spite of the darkness. The floor in the room shines. George goes to the bedroom. The shades are down in the bedroom. It's dark therefore. The light switch in the bedroom is on the right of the door. George turns on the light. It's weak. It's in the middle of the ceiling. The light seems yellow like an old sheet of paper. The color of the light seems to be due to age. There's a bed, two bedside cabinets, two lamps, two chairs, and a chest of drawers in the bedroom. The right side of the bed faces George. There's one bedside cabinet on each side of the bed. There's a lamp on each of the bedside cabinets. George goes up to the right side of the bed. He opens the door of the cabinet. He has to kneel down to do this. The inside of the cabinet is divided in half by a shelf. George empties his pockets. He puts the things from the pockets onto the shelf. The only thing he doesn't put there are his keys. He puts them on top of the cabinet. He takes off his wrist watch. He puts it also on top of the cabinet. He's wearing a suit, turtleneck, undershorts, socks, and shoes. He takes off his jacket. He throws it on top of the bed. He takes off the turtleneck. He folds it. He does this on the bed. The chest of drawers is on his right. George takes the turtleneck. He goes to the chest of drawers. He puts the turtleneck in the bottom drawer. He goes back to the bed. He picks up the jacket. He goes to the empty room. The shades are also down in this room. It's therefore also largely dark. The light switch in this room is on the left of the door. George turns on the light. It's warm. It makes the room cozy. This is so in spite of the room's being empty. There's a closet on the left of the door. George goes up to the closet. He opens it. He hangs the jacket on a hanger in the closet. He takes off his shoes. There are shoe pockets on the inside of the door. George puts the shoes in them. He takes off his pants. He hangs them up on a pant hanger in the closet. He hangs them up next to the jacket. He takes off his socks. He puts them inside a pair of shoes in the shoe pockets. The socks hang down from the shoes. The socks look limp. George takes off his undershorts. He puts them on the shelf in the closet. He's naked. He feels a little cold. The cold makes him feel feverish. There's a pair of Japanese thong sandals lying on the floor in the closet. They're rubber. They're white. George puts them on. He closes the closet. He turns off the light. He leaves the room. He goes to the attic door. He has a chinning bar in the attic. The bar is laid across the stairwell in the attic. George had laid the bar there himself. He'd fastened the bar by nailing a piece of board on each side of the ends of the bar. He's planning to chin himself. There's a key in the door. The key is of the old-fashioned type. The door is locked. George unlocks it. He opens it. There's a light switch on the left. George switches the light on. It's high up in the attic. The light is weak. It seems very distant. It's like the memory of something. This something seems dear. George looks up. He sees the bar. He sees the roof above it. The roof is made of boards. They're illuminated by the light. They're rough. They look orange in the light. The sight is beautiful. It's warm. It makes George feel less cold. The roof looks like the sky. The sky seems made of wood. George lowers his head. He walks up four steps. From these steps he can reach the chinning bar. He raises his arms. He grabs the chinning bar with his hands. He looks at them. Their flesh bulges in a few places as they close. The hands look like the cheeks of a person having taken something large in his mouth. George's hands seem mouths that'd swallowed the bar. The hands seem very strong because of that. George is pleased by this. He's glad at a part of himself looking so strong. He tenses the muscles of his arms and chest. He gets ready for the exercise. He lifts himself up. He lifts himself until his chin rises above the bar. He does this with little effort. He then lowers himself down. He does this slowly. He bends his knees on letting himself down. He does this in order to let himself down as far as possible. He repeats the chinning process nineteen more times. The process gets strenuous from the seventeenth repetition on. The twentieth repetition is especially strenuous. George isn't sure he'll complete it. He does this however. He could chin himself a few more times in reality. The reason for the twentieth repetition being so strenuous is psychological. George had decided to chin himself twenty times only. He chins himself twenty times every day. The chinning exercise is one of a long series he does every day. He exercises between two and three hours a day. About one hour of this is dedicated to running. George is panting on finishing chinning himself. His arms feel heavy. They feel muscular. George no longer feels cold. He doesn't feel hot however. He's merely not aware of the temperature. In other words, he's comfortable. He goes out of the attic. He turns off the light. He shuts the door. He locks it. He does this for no one to hide in the attic during his being away. He walks into the bedroom. He shrugs his shoulders. He shakes his arms. He does this to loosen up. He breathes heavily. He walks back and forth for about half a minute. He stays on the right side of the bed. He then goes into the hallway. He goes toward the staircase landing. He goes into the study. He turns on the lamp there. It's near the table. The light is soft. It's yellowish. It's like a warm personality. George is comforted by the light. He goes to the cot. He opens his attache case. There's a stack of loose pages in it. There are about twenty of them. About half of them are handwritten and half typed. This is part of a manuscript George is working on. The manuscript is a work of fiction. The part is a chapter. The chapter is the last one in the book. George has finished the first draft of the chapter. He's typing it up. He typed the pages up the previous night. He took them to work to proofread them. He did this throughout the day a few pages at a time. He did this instead of breaks. He picks up the pages. There's a closet on the left of the door. George keeps some of his writing there. He goes to the closet. He opens it. There are shelves in it. The rest of the manuscript lies on top of one of the shelves. George puts the pages with the rest of the manuscript. He separates the handwritten pages from the typed ones first. The manuscript is already separated this way. George puts the two kinds of pages in the proper places. He closes the closet. He goes back to the attache case. He closes it. He picks it up. He goes to the credenza. He lays the attache case on top of it. By now he's recovered completely from the chinning. One of the chairs in the room stands by the table. The other chair stands in one of the corners. George gets the chair in the corner. He brings the chair to the table. He sets the chair down about two feet from the other chair. The backs of the chairs face each other. The backs are straight. George gets in between the chairs. He puts one of his hands on top of each of the backs of the chairs. He faces the writing chest. He lifts his feet. He supports himself on his arms. He lowers himself almost as far as possible. He bends his knees in the process. He then lifts himself as far as possible. He repeats the process nineteen more times. He does this quite fast. He doesn't find the exercise strenuous. This is true even of the last few repetitions. George could repeat the process many more times. He's breathing a little heavier after the exercise than before it however. He puts his feet down on the floor. He takes the second chair back to the corner. He goes back to the lamp. He turns it off. He goes into the bathroom. The light switch in the bathroom is on the right of the door. George turns on the light. It's in the middle of the ceiling. The light is strong. It's white. It seems a blank sheet of paper. The light seems a little unpleasant to George because of this. He feels an urge to urinate. The lid of the toilet bowl is down. George raises the lid. He urinates in the bowl. He flushes the toilet. He watches the water go down the drain. He lowers the lid on the toilet bowl. He goes up to the sink. He turns on the hot water. It's cold however. This is due to no one having used the hot water during the day. The water has grown cold in the pipes. There's a soap dish next to the sink. There's a bar of soap there. George takes it. He washes his hands with soap and water. He puts the soap back in its original place. He rinses his hands. He turns off the water. It hadn't grown warm by then. There's a towel rack next to the sink. There are two towels there. One of them is a bath towel. The other one is a hand towel. George takes the hand towel. He dries his hands on it. He hangs it back in its original place. He closes the drain in the sink. He takes his contact lenses out over the sink. This was the reason for his closing the drain. He was afraid of a lens falling down the drain. He puts the lenses in the case. He takes the right lens out first. He always does this in this order. There's a medicine cabinet above the sink. There are shelves there. George puts the lens case on the top shelf. He closes the cabinet. There's a bathtub and shower in the bathroom. There's a rod running along the free edge of the bathtub about seven feet up. There's a bath mat hanging over the free edge of the bathtub. George puts the bath mat on the floor next to the bathtub. He sticks his hand in behind the shower curtain. He turns on the hot water in the shower. He turns on the shower quite strong. He takes his sandals off. He leaves them next to the bath mat. He steps onto it. The bathroom has a window. The window is of the casement type. The window opens out. George opens it a little. He does this to let the steam out of the bathroom when the steam starts gathering. He's waiting for the water to turn warm. He turns toward the mirror. He looks at himself in the mirror. His face is tanned. George thinks it looks childish. He feels vulnerable. The water coming out of the shower makes a lot of noise. At this time the sound of the water changes. The pitch of the sound rises. This is due to the water having become warm. George knows the meaning of the rising pitch. He gets into the bathtub. He doesn't stand under the shower. The water is falling only on his legs and feet. It's fairly hot. George turns on the cold water. He does this until the temperature of the water seems right to him. He actually makes the water almost cold. He feels however the temperature will be right when the hot water reaches its highest temperature. His judgement will prove right. George remembers the previous night. That night he'd taken a bath. He almost never takes a bath. He takes showers. The reason for his having taken a bath is the following. George had had diarrhea for about four months. His rectum had gotten sore from the diarrhea. His rectum had bled sometimes. George was worried about this. He thought he had cancer of the rectum. He went to see his doctor in connection with the rectum. The doctor gave George pills for diarrhea. The doctor also ordered George's stool to be analyzed. This was done. George's stool turned out to have a parasite in it. The parasite didn't have to cause diarrhea. The parasite could have done this however. George was treated for the parasite. The diarrhea didn't stop. George's stool was analyzed again. The parasite was still there. George was treated for the parasite again. Coincidentally with the second treatment the diarrhea stopped. George's rectum had become less painful prior to this. With the diarrhea's going away the rectum got very sore. This was due to the stool becoming harder. The rectum bled quite frequently. George went to see his doctor again. George was afraid even more he had cancer of the rectum. The doctor examined George's rectum. He found a fissure in it. He assured George George didn't have cancer. George's fears were allayed. The doctor prescribed some suppositories with cortizone in them, drinking prune juice for loosening the stool, and hot baths as a cure for the fissure. George followed the first cure consistently. The second two cures he followed only intermittently. This was due to his not having time to buy prune juice at first, forgetting to drink prune juice later, and not having time for and not liking to take baths. George had followed the cure for thirteen days. He'd taken a bath only twice during that time. He'd turned the water off when the bathtub was about two-thirds full while taking the bath the previous night. The water looked greenish. It seemed ghastly. It was like the face of a corpse. It was quiet in the bathroom. George put his right foot in the water. The water was disturbed. It made noises. They were faint. They were audible however. They sounded pleasant. They sounded like a very distant chiming of bells. George put his left foot in the water. He stood in the bathtub. The water was hot. George was afraid to lower himself into the water. He began lowering himself however. He was submerging in the water. He seemed to be doing this with great difficulty. He seemed a wedge being driven into a block of wood. He also seemed to be lowering himself into the water painfully. He seemed a large splinter being driven into human flesh. The flesh seemed his. George remembers this now. He finds the memory unpleasant. He tries to forget it. He tries to concentrate on the present. He steps under the shower. He closes his eyes. He feels the water beating down on his body. He feels the water spreading over his body. The water seems like many fingers. They seem long. They seem thin. They seem to belong to one hand. The hand seems friendly. George runs his hand over his body. His body seems slippery. The water seems viscous. It seems oily. George moves around under the shower. At one point his movement causes pain in his rectum. The pain is faint. It worries George however. He becomes aware of his fear of having cancer. He turns his back to the shower. He lets the water run down over his anus. He hopes this will serve the same purpose as the bath. He's aware however he'd have to stand this way for a long time. He knows he won't do it. He tries not to become conscious of this. He begins to rub his body more to take his attention away from the preceding thought. He does this for a few seconds. There's a towel rack over the bathtub. A washcloth hangs on the rack. George takes the washcloth. He wets it. There's a soap dish in the wall next to the bathtub. There's a bar of soap in the dish. There's a handle above the soap dish. George hangs the washcloth on the handle. He decides to soap himself. He turns off the water. He takes the soap out of the dish. He soaps his whole body. He puts the soap away. He takes the washcloth. He turns on the hot and cold water. He regulates the water to the previous temperature. He stands under the shower. He washes himself with the washcloth. He washes all the soap off his body. He wrings the washcloth out. He hangs it up on the rack. He turns off the hot water. He turns up the cold water. The water turns cold. The jets of water seem to become solid to George. They seem to pass through his body like semirigid rods. The rods seem steel. George feels like St. Sebastian. George turns around under the shower. This seems painful to him because of his feeling like St. Sebastian. It's as if George had to pull out the steel rods in order to turn. It's also as if new steel rods had to pierce his body then in order for him to continue feeling like St. Sebastian. George rubs his body with his hands. He does both of these acts fast. He turns off the water. He pushes back the shower curtain. He feels refreshed. He feels full of energy. He steps out onto the bath mat. He looks in the mirror. It's steamed up. The bathroom is cold. There's a cold draft coming in through the window. George takes the bath towel off the rack. He wipes off the mirror. He sees himself reflected in it. He again thinks his face looks childish. He proceeds drying himself. In a few seconds the mirror steams up again. George again wipes it off. He seems to be unable to dry himself with the mirror being steamed up. It's as if he were constantly looking in the mirror watching himself drying himself. This is so in spite of his taking only an occasional glance at himself in the mirror while drying himself and, moreover, seeing only his face and shoulders in the mirror. George finishes drying himself. He hangs the towel up on the rack. He puts on his sandals. He hangs up the bath mat on the bathtub. He turns off the light. He walks out of the bathroom. He closes the door. He heads for the empty room. He turns on the light there. He goes to the closet. He opens it. There's a pair of pajamas hanging there. George puts them on. He takes off his sandals. He puts them in their original place. He puts on his socks. There's a pair of slippers on the floor in the closet. George puts them on. There's a bathrobe hanging in the closet. George puts the bathrobe on. He closes the closet. He turns off the light. He goes to the bedroom. He puts his watch on. He takes the keys. He puts them in one of the bathrobe pockets. He turns off the light. He goes into the hallway. He turns on the light at the bottom landing. He walks downstairs. He turns off the light at the top landing. The living room is off the hallway at the bottom of the stairs. George goes to the living room. There's a stereo set there. It's in a cabinet. George goes up to the cabinet. He opens it. He turns on the radio. It's transistorized. It's tuned in to a rock station. The volume is turned up fairly high. George leaves it like this. The music has a strong beat. George likes the music. He goes back into the hallway. He turns off the light at the bottom of the landing. He's in near-darkness again. He can see fairly well however. This is due to the light coming in from the street through the windows in the room next to the kitchen. George walks to the kitchen. He decides to have eggs, tomato salad, and bread for supper. He decides to scramble the eggs. He goes to the refrigerator.

He opens it. He takes a container of milk, box of eggs, and a bar of butter out of the refrigerator. He puts them on top of the cabinet. He opens the cabinet. There are cooking dishes there. There's a skillet among them. George takes the skillet. He takes the butter. He goes over to the stove. He puts the skillet on one of the burners. The stove is electric. George turns the burner on. He sets it to the highest setting. He opens one of the drawers in the cabinet next to the stove. There are cooking utensils there. George takes a spatula out of the drawer. He closes the drawer. He puts the spatula down near the burner. He goes back to the refrigerator. He opens it. He takes two tomatoes out of it. He closes it. There are cabinets on the wall next to the refrigerator. George opens one of them. There are dishes there. George takes out a salad plate. He closes the cabinet. He puts the plate on top of the bottom cabinet. He puts the tomatoes next to the plate. They look pale. They look like rubber balls. George goes to the drawer next to the stove. He opens the drawer. He takes a kitchen knife out of it. He goes back to the plate. He takes a tomato. He slices is crosswise. The slices are fairly thick. George custs the tomato into five slices. There are empty spaces inside the tomato. They look black. They look like cavities in teeth. George arranges the slices along the edge of the plate. They rest over each other. George repeats the process with the second tomato. There's a bottle of salad oil in the cabinet under the sink. George gets the bottle. He pours some oil over the tomatoes. He puts the bottle back in its place. There's a bottle of vinegar in the refrigerator. George gets the bottle. He pours some vinegar over the tomatoes. He puts the bottle back in its place. There's a salt-and-pepper shaker in the cabinet behind him. He gets the shaker. He grinds some pepper over the tomatoes. He pours some salt over them. He leaves the shaker on top of the cabinet. He looks at the stove. The burner under the skillet is red-hot. George walks quickly over to the stove. He takes the spatula. He cuts some butter off from the bar with the spatula. He drops the butter in the skillet. The butter begins to smoke. The smoke rises in thin wisps. They're white. The butter crackles in the skillet. The smell of burning butter spreads through the air. George is worried about the butter. He looks at the skillet. He sees the lump of butter dwindling quickly. He opens the egg carton. He takes an egg. He breaks it on the edge of the skillet. He drops the egg in the skillet. The crackling in the skillet gets very loud. The crackling seems spoken words full of vowels. It also seems loud laughter. George puts the egg shell on top of the cabinet. He repeats the process with two more eggs. He takes the milk carton. He pours some milk into the skillet.

He pours about a third of a cup. This stops the crackling. George gets the spatula. He stirs the eggs and milk. The milk blends in with the eggs. They get hard very quickly. They form lumps. The lumps are elongated. They're pale. They look like shelled shrimp. The lumps also look like tattered clothes. The clothes seem very tattered. Soon all the eggs in the skillet are transformed into these lumps. The bottom of the skillet is dry. The bottom is black. It's shiny. It looks like a clear sky at night with some stars in it. George is disappointed by the texture of the eggs. He likes his eggs moist. He's been trying to cook eggs moist for himself for about eight months. He knows eggs become hard when the skillet is too hot. He hasn't succeeded in cooking eggs to his satisfaction even once however. He always gets the skillet so hot the eggs become hard. He takes the skillet off the burner. The handle of the skillet is hot. George gives a hiss. He curses silently. He's disgusted. He puts the skillet on top of the stove. He gets a plate out of the cabinet next to the refrigerator. He goes to the skillet. He puts the eggs on the plate with the help of the spatula. He looks at the plate with tomatoes. He realizes they would fit onto the plate with the eggs. He gets the plate with tomatoes. He brings the plate with tomatoes to the plate with the eggs. He pushes the tomatoes onto the plate with eggs with the help of the spatula. The tomatoes fall in a heap. They don't form a pattern. The oil and vinegar flow over in between the eggs. At this instant the eggs look like a ruin to George. The ruin seems very old. It seems Roman. This is probably due to the paleness of the eggs. They look like marble. At this instant George realizes he's forgotten to salt the eggs. He again curses silently. He gets the salt-and-pepper shaker. He pours some salt over the eggs. He turns the eggs over with the spatula. He pours more salt over them. He grinds some pepper over them. It's as if he were grinding his teeth. There's a drawer in the cupboard next to the refrigerator. George goes to the drawer. He gets a knife and fork from it. He gets a napkin from the cupboard under the sink. He goes over to the plate with the food. He takes the plate. He goes to the room off the kitchen. There's a table there. It stands against the wall on the right. George puts the plate, knife, fork, and napkin on the table. He puts the knife on the right side of the plate. He puts the fork and napkin on the left side. He turns on the light in the room. He goes into the kitchen. He goes to the refrigerator. There's bread in it. The bread is of the Komisbrot type. The bread is sealed in plastic. George gets the bread. He goes into the room next to the kitchen. He goes to the table. There are two chairs next to it. One of them is in front of the plate with the food. George sits down on that chair. He opens the package of bread. He takes out a slice of bread. He begins to eat. The eggs are insipid. They seem plastic. The tomatoes are hard. They crunch. They seem frozen. They also seem glass. The vinegar is very sharp. It seems a razor blade. The bread is dry. It seems sawdust. George tries not to think about the food. He tries to think about things other than eating. He remembers a half-finished bottle of wine he has. The wine is red. George had opened the bottle when having visitors. This was about a week ago. George thinks the wine will turn acid soon. He thinks he should drink it. He decides not to do this. He feels a keen pleasure at this. The sensation is like that derived from seeing a culprit being punished. George feels the pleasure for a few minutes. He then forgets about it. This is the only pleasure he derives from the meal. He finished the meal thinking about various things. They have to do with his personal life. They don't follow a pattern. George's thoughts are like a pile of jumbled-up objects. George gets up from the table. He takes the plate, knife, fork, and napkin. He goes to the kitchen. He puts the things on top of the cabinet on the right side of the sink. He stops by the sink. He looks at it. His eyes however aren't focused on it. He stands this way for about thirty seconds. He's not thinking about anything in particular. He then realizes what he's doing. He collects himself. He turns on the hot water. There's a sponge next to the faucet. George takes the sponge. He puts it under the water. The water is still cold. George waits for it to get warm. When cold, it's unpleasant. It's like a harsh personality. The water gets warm slowly. Eventually it's noticeably warm. It's pleasant then. It's like a warm personality. The person seems to have gotten friendly gradually. George kneads the sponge under the water. He soaks up some water in the sponge. He turns off the water. He goes to the room off the kitchen. He wipes the table off with the sponge. The sponge leaves a layer of water on the table. The layer glitters. The glittering imparts an appearance of elegance to the table. George returns to the kitchen. He puts the sponge next to the faucet. He turns on the hot water. He stacks the dishes and utensils in the sink. He washes them. The water gets quite hot at one point. George has to make the water cooler by turning on the cold water. In the middle of doing the dishes George gets a liquid-soap bottle from under the sink. This is when he's doing the salad plate. It's oily. George uses the soap on it. From then on he uses the soap on the remainder of the things in the sink. He puts the washed things on the left side of the sink. He puts the plates and skillet face down. Having finished the dishes he turns off the water. There's a towel rack under the cabinet next to the refrigerator. There's a towel hanging on the rack. George gets the towel. He dries the things with it. He puts the dry things in their original places. He puts the liquid soap in its original place on having dried all the things. He gets a container of cleanser from under the sink. He pours some cleanser into the sink. He puts the container back in its place. He turns on the hot water. He gets the sponge. He washes the sink with it. He rinses out the sponge. He turns off the water. He cleans the top of the stove. He wipes off the tops of the cabinets on both sides of the sink. He squeezes out the sponge. He puts the sponge in its original place. He looks straight ahead. There's a window above the sink. The window has a ledge up above. There are flowerpots on the ledge and the sill. There's also one flowerpot hanging down from the ceiling in front of the window. There are different types of ferns growing in the flowerpots. George looks at the ferns. Most of them look bad. Some of them are obviously dying. The dead parts of the ferns are pale. The dead parts are nearly white. They look like faded handwriting written in ink. The handwriting seems to deal with emotions. It could be love letters for instance. The love letters seem to be connected with George. He could have written or received them. He's not sure why the ferns are dying. He suspects this is due to his not watering them enough. This is so again in spite of his watering them twice a week. He feels he should water them now. He however decides against it. This produces in him the same emotion as deciding not to drink the wine. Soon he ceases being aware of the ferns. He stares at them absentmindedly. He stands like this for about a minute. He again realizes what he's doing. He collects himself again. He turns away from the sink. He turns off the light in the kitchen. He goes to the room off the kitchen. He turns off the light there. He's in near darkness again. He enters the hallway. He goes to the staircase landing. He turns on the light at the bottom and top landings. He goes into the living room. He turns off the radio. He goes back into the hallway. He's about to climb the stairs. He then remembers the thermostat. He remembers having turned it up. He doesn't want to leave it turned up while he's asleep. He's not planning to go to sleep immediately on going upstairs. He doesn't feel like going downstairs once he's upstairs however. He therefore decides to turn the thermostat down now. This is so in spite of the fact it'll get colder in the house. George is aware of this fact. This produces in him the same emotion as not drinking the wine and not watering the ferns. This in turn makes him want even more to turn down the thermostat. He goes into the room off the kitchen. He goes up to the thermostat. He turns it all the way down. He does this without having to look at it. This is the reason for his not having turned on the light in the room. George goes back into the hallway. He goes to the staircase landing. He climbs the stairs. He climbs them two at a time. He moves fast. He looks energetic. He goes into his study. He opens the writing closet. He gets some typing paper and the manuscript of the chapter he's working on. He goes into the second room off the staircase landing. There's a light on the wall on the right of the door. George turns on the light. It's bright. It's unpleasant. It's like an unpleasant personality. George seems to especially dislike this type of personality. There's a table, lamp, typewriter and two chairs in the room. The table is round. It stands in the middle of the room. One of the chairs stands next to the table. The other chair stands in one of the corners of the room. The lamp and the typewriter are on the table. The typewriter is electric. It has a cover on it. George goes up to the table. He turns on the lamp. The light is strong. It's pleasant however. It's like a pleasant strong personality. George seems to especially like this type of personality. He puts the paper and manuscript down on the table. He puts the manuscript on the left of the typewriter. He puts the paper in the middle of the table. There's a drawer in the left side of the table. George opens the drawer. There's a pencil and eraser there. George takes them. He closes the drawer. He puts the pencil on the right side of the typewriter. He puts the eraser on the right side of the pencil. He does this to prevent the pencil from rolling off the table. He takes the cover off the typewriter. He goes to the chair in the corner. He puts the cover down on the chair. He goes back to the table. He gets two sheets of paper. He puts them in the typewriter. He uses two sheets instead of one to prevent the platen from deteriorating. The typed pages are on top of the handwritten ones. George takes the typed pages. He puts them face down next to the paper. He turns the last page over. The number at the top of that page is 264. George remembers the number. He looks at the bottom of the page. The words there are "he hasn't." George remembers the words. He sits down at the typewriter. He looks at the manuscript. The top page is where he'd left off typing. The spot is marked with a pencil. George looks at the spot. The words there correspond to the words on the bottom of the typed page. George is pleased by this. He turns on the typewriter. He types his initial and last name on the left side. He types the number 265 in the middle. He types the title of the chapter on the right side. He starts a new line. He proceeds typing off the handwritten page. He touch-types. He types fast. He makes many mistakes however. He's aware of most of them. He rarely stops to correct them however. This is due to the typing being a rough draft. George will have the final typing done by a professional typist. The handwritten page is quadrille. The handwriting on the page is written with a ball-point pen. The handwriting is small. It's very hard to read. Even George has trouble reading it. Sometimes he has to stop to decipher a word. He frequently leans down toward the page then. This is due to his not wearing his contact lenses. George finishes typing the page. It's covered with print from top to bottom. There's no space left at the bottom. The page contains many more words than a normal typed page. George puts the typed page down on top of the typed pages. He puts the page face down. He keeps the clean sheet. He takes another sheet of paper. He puts the two sheets in the typewriter. He proceeds typing. He follows the same procedure as with the first page. He types this way for about an hour and a half. He types eight pages. He felt tired after the second page. He'd debated whether or not to stop then. He'd decided to go on. He still hasn't finished the chapter. There are another four handwritten pages to be typed. George feels tired however. He decides to stop. He turns off the typewriter. He marks the spot where he'd stopped with the pencil. The last words he'd typed are "pages to be typed." He stands up. He feels stiff. He nearly reels. He takes the paper out of the typewriter. He puts the typed page on top of the typed pages. He puts the clean page on top of the stack of paper. He takes the eraser. He puts the pencil and eraser in the drawer. He goes to the chair in the corner. He takes the typewriter cover. He goes back to the table. He puts the cover on the typewriter. He puts the typed part of the manuscript on top of the handwritten one. He puts the clean typing paper on top of the manuscript. He takes the stack of paper. He turns off the lamp on the table. He turns off the lamp by the door. He goes out of the room. He goes into his study. He puts the typing paper and manuscript in the closet. He goes to his attache case. He opens it. There's a folder inside it. There's writing paper and pens in the folder. George uses the folder for keeping his current writing in. He takes the folder. He squats down. He opens the credenza. There are books in it. George takes one of them. It's the history of Ukrainian literature by Dmytro Chyzhevs'kyj. The book is in Ukrainian. George closes the credenza. He stands up. He goes to his bedroom. He turns on the lamp on the bedside cabinet near the door. The light isn't very strong. It's warm. It's like a quiet personality. George also seems to especially like this type of personality. He puts the folder and book on top of the cabinet. He goes to the bathroom. He turns on the light there. He brushes his teeth. He lifts the toilet seat. He urinates in the toilet bowl. He flushes the toilet. He puts the toilet seat down. He washes his hands with soap. He washes his face just with water. He dries his face and hands with the hand towel on the towel rack. He turns off the light. He goes out of the bathroom. He closes the door. He turns off the light at the top of the staircase. He goes to the empty room. He takes the keys out of the robe pocket. He keeps them in his right hand. He takes off the robe. He hangs it up in the closet. He takes off his slippers. He puts them on the floor in the closet. He takes off his socks. He puts them in a pair of shoes in the shoe pockets. He puts on the rubber sandals. He closes the closet. He walks out of the room. There's a linen closet in the hallway on the right of the room. George opens the closet. There's a quilt there. George takes it. He closes the linen closet. He goes to his bedroom. The bed is made for sleeping. George puts the quilt over the bed. He squats down. He opens the bedside cabinet. He puts the keys on the shelf. He closes the cabinet. He stands up. He takes off his watch. He puts it on top of the cabinet. He sits down on the edge of the bed. He takes off the sandals. He puts them by the side of the bed. He puts them neatly together. Their toes point at the door. George climbs in under the covers. He turns left. He moves over to the left side of the bed. There's a phone on top of the cabinet there. George looks at the phone. It's a standard model. The phone is black. It shines in places. It resembles a closed mouth. George keeps a radio in the cabinet. He opens the door of the cabinet. This cabinet is divided by a shelf as the other one. The radio is on the shelf. George reaches for the on/off knob. He turns on the radio. It's a tube model. A humming sound is heard on the radio's being turned on. The sound continues for some fifteen seconds. It's then replaced by that of music. The music is rock. The radio is tuned in to the same station as the one downstairs. George waits to see if the radio is properly tuned in. It is. George moves back to the right side of the bed. There are two pillows on the bed. George takes the pillow from the left side. He puts that pillow on top of the pillow on the right side. He sits up a little. He lies back on the pillows. He takes the book. He opens it. He leafs through it. He comes to the chapter on classicism. He starts reading. He reads the introduction a few times. He finds it interesting. He finds it concise. He goes on to the rest of the chapter. He's unaware of the music. At one point he becomes aware of it. The music bothers him. He finds it too emotionally disturbing. He decides to find some classical music. He puts the book down on the bed. He moves over to the left side of the bed. He finds the dial knob. He turns it. He turns it to a classical station he knows. There's a man talking on this station. George decides to leave the radio tuned in to the station. He likes most of the music played on that station. He moves back to the right side of the bed. He picks up the book. He continues reading. The man on the radio announces the next piece to be played. The piece is a baroque composition. George prefers baroque music to all other classical music. He's pleased. He finishes reading the chapter on classicism. This brings him over to the chapter on romanticism. He proceeds reading the chapter. He reads the introduction. He reads it slowly. He finds it also very interesting. He finds it also very concise. He feels he's learned something about romanticism. This is so in spite of his having read the book before as well as other books on romanticism. This is due to his having forgotten the information. George has come now to the body of the chapter. He'd be reading about Ukrainian romanticism next. He doesn't like romanticist writing. Besides, he feels tired. He decides not to read any more. By then the baroque composition is over. Another piece of music is playing. George hadn't heard what the piece is. The piece definitely is from the nineteenth century however. George doesn't like music from this period. He decides to go to sleep. He puts the book on top of the cabinet on the right. There's an alarm clock on top of the cabinet. The clock is electric. George picks it up. He looks at it. It's set for a little before seven. George decides this is the right hour for him to get up. He pulls out the alarm knob. He puts the clock back on top of the cabinet. He turns off the light. Momentarily he can't see anything. The dial of the radio is illuminated. The light is fairly strong. After a short while therefore George sees the outlines of the room. He leans over to the left side of the bed. He sees the phone. It still looks like a closed mouth. The phone however also looks now like closed eyes. George finds both these images depressing. He takes his eyes off the phone. He tries not to think about it. He's not aware of these acts and emotions. He reaches with his hand for the on/off knob. He finds the knob. He turns it. The radio makes a click. The light goes out.